# BLOOD BROTHERS

**Archbarnes.com**

**ISBN: 978-0-6151-5051-2**

## Dedication

Anyone who writes a novel takes license with facts. Otherwise, extremely technical and esoteric subject matter would become boring. Law enforcement has become a challenging science, and law enforcement agencies regularly perform miracles in solving crimes that are made more difficult by various constraints and legal interpretations of the rights of suspects. While I cherish the freedoms and rights we all too often take for granted, I am constantly reminded that our law enforcement officers are the last line of protection against deviant and brutal individuals who lurk in the shadows created by some of those same freedoms. I dedicate this novel to all those who **"serve and protect."**

## Acknowledgment

As always, I could not have completed this project without the direct help and the indirect support of my wonderful wife, Judy. She is, and always has been, my source of inspiration, my *raison d'etre.*

AKB

Other Novels in the Arnold Towncraft Series:

Old Dogs, New Tricks

In for a Penny

Unconscious

Look for the next in this series, coming soon.

Arch Barnes is a former executive with a Fortune 500 Corporation and an award-winning university professor. In addition to this crime series, he is compiling (with co-author Jack Marlando) an historical series of novels that tell of America's social, economic & political evolution, 1776 to the present day. The overarching title of that series is *American Tapestry.*

# Blood Brothers

**Chapter One**

Bryan Olmstead looked around the crowded cafeteria, searching, but not exactly sure what for, and he scowled. This place, located in the San Diego county courthouse, was lousy with cops. Cops and lawyers, talking fancy legal talk and laughing a lot. No doubt laughing at the games they played, using the system to screw anyone who was not a lawyer or a cop. Fooling around with people's lives, suing each other for big bucks, making claims of all kinds, with slime-ball attorneys on both sides of every case getting their fat fee no matter which way it was decided. And there were the criminal cases, cops framing innocent people, and worse. As far as Bryan was concerned the so-called justice system was a private club, and outsiders were always screwed every which-way. He already hated his own lawyer, though he'd met the man only twice. Hated him mostly because he was what he was, but also because of his obvious prejudice. A young public defender, Darvin Schwartz made it plain that he was convinced of his client's guilt right from the start, so Bryan felt doomed, screwed by the system that claimed fairness and justice for all. *Hah!*

Bryan's obvious guilt he chose to see as irrelevant; he had brutally raped and slaughtered three young women, for no reason other than to satisfy his own bestial urges, but this fact was just a mere detail having nothing to do with how bad the system was. "Nothing in this screwed-up world is fair!" he said with venom. His muttered comment attracted the attention of another prisoner, a mere youth, seated at the opposite end of the table they shared in this courtroom cafe. There were just the two of them at this table for six. The four empty chairs had not attracted others, not to this table. Most of the places at the other tables in this long, narrow room were occupied by lawyers, clerical people, witnesses, jurors and police officers of one sort or another.

"You got that right!" the young man said, eying Bryan coldly.

Bryan realized his angry utterance had produced this question and he now regretted opening his mouth, especially in here. He had always been vocal about a number of things, when alone or in the company of others, muttering things intended not as conversation but just simply venting or ranting. In his cell, over these last few days, after a period of six weeks being "evaluated" at the Patton State Hospital, near San Bernardino, he'd been unusually noisy. The attendants there–they chose not to call them "guards"–had asked him to knock it off a few times, but he'd not listened to them. It somehow made him feel good to shout, or just speak out, using language he knew they would find infuriating: "Your stinking government bureaucracy is out of control," he would yell, or "The entire system is screwed up, is in need of serious reform. The fat cats in business and government get away with murder while the little guy gets the shaft."

Bryan felt sure he was brighter than most people. The State Hospital psychologist had confirmed it, in fact, with several different intelligence and aptitude tests. He had always been bright and clever at many different things, but he had been unwilling or unable to use his intellect in anything more productive than devising ways to beat the system. He was especially filled with hatred toward women; in fact this seemed to be his primary motivation. "They're all whores and conniving bitches," he would often say. "Liars and cheats, and they're far more brutish than any man!"

Yes, Bryan Olmstead hated women more than anything, and he'd known it for a long time. He saw plenty of them in this room right now as he glanced around again, hoping his companion at the table would not attempt to make conversation. There was no point.

The women around Bryan were lawyers, female deputies, females of all kinds! On the one hand he wanted to use these women for his pleasure, but then again he hated them so much he couldn't stand to be near them. With his left hand he wiped away the drool that had oozed from one corner of his mouth and he turned back to the kid at the end of the table.

"So what's your rap?" the youngster said.

"What's it to you?" Bryan said, with no particular emotion.

"Hey, man, no big deal. Just trying to be friendly is all. I saw you come in here with two deputies. I rated only one, so I know they got you for something big. You kill somebody?"

The guy was maybe eighteen, no more. He had steel-gray eyes that penetrated in a scary way, but the left eye drifted a little, making it hard to tell if he was looking at you or somewhere else.

"Think you're pretty smart, don't you?" Bryan said.

"I seen you come in here with them two badges, and that tells me something, but that ain't all. I reckon I seen your face in the papers. Yeah, you're the one that killed and raped them women, ain'cha? Was it three or four?"

At that point one of the two deputies who had escorted Bryan to the court approached the table. She had been in the cafeteria lineup with her partner, checking out the menu board. "What do you want to drink with your sandwich, Bryan?" she said coldly. "They got soft drinks, juice, milk, iced tea, hot tea, hot chocolate and coffee, so what'll it be?"

"Juice," Bryan said, matching the deputy's tone. "Any kind."

She turned and walked back toward the others and Bryan eyed her ample rear end lasciviously. He then turned back to the other prisoner and noticed that the two of them had several things in common. Both of them had ill-fitting polyester suits, bought for them by "the system." Dressed this way, the theory went, a judge or a jury would not form a negative first impression. *Like Hell they wouldn't!* A half-decent suit, a haircut and a fresh shave made even the most hardened criminal look innocent... or so some people thought. Bryan knew he cleaned up pretty well, though. His mother had always told him he was a "good looking boy." *Yeah? Then why did you and your drunken boyfriend always kick the crap out of me? For nothing!* He felt his anger on the rise as he thought of his mother. He didn't swear openly, not ever. Oh, he knew plenty of curse words, and under his breath he used them often. As a boy he'd used them openly, all the time, but he'd taken so many beatings for it that ultimately, and even today, if he uttered any of the most common four-letter words he would involuntarily wet his pants a little. The irony was that the mother who beat him for cursing, and her ex-marine boyfriend–who had been kicked out of the service for immoral conduct–both swore like oil rig workers; especially when they had been drinking... which was all the time.

The other thing he had in common with this wild-eyed and nosy kid was that they were both handcuffed to the leg of the table. Bryan leaned to one side and let his eye examine the leg to which the young prisoner's wrist was manacled. He confirmed his suspicion: as was the case with his own, the table leg was lag-bolted to the concrete floor. The table itself was made of steel, but it wasn't so heavy a man couldn't lift it enough to ease out the open end of the manacle. Bolted down, however, there was no way.

"So what are *you* charged with?" Bryan said. "Stealing candy bars?"

Bryan's sarcasm was met with a smile so bright it surprised him.

"Yeah, right! A candy bar!" He tossed his blonde ragged hair in defiance, adding, "Come to think of it, there was a

9

chocolate bar inside the Lexie I ripped off. How did you know that?"

"Lexie?"

The kid smiled again. "Lexus. The big mother."

"Big deal!" Bryan said. He glanced over at the counter, where it looked like his deputies were being served. "So you took a Lexus for a joy ride, huh? Well ain't you the brave kid."

Again the Cheshire cat grin, and the eyebrows raised high. "The Lexus I took belonged to the San Diego Mayor, but that wasn't the fun part. I drove it all the way up to Los Angeles before they caught me. Got that sucker up to one-thirty at times, with five cruisers chasing me all the way up the five freeway. Highway Patrol. But this was the big momma Lexus, like I said. The V-8. Man, does that sucker fly! They say I caused a couple of serious accidents, so I'm charged with something called reckless endangerment and half a dozen other things. Ain't them fancy words? Reckless endangerment."

The pride he showed in this act of foolishness and all-too-obvious show of bravado amplified the antisocial nature of this young delinquent.

Deputy Walsh showed up again and placed Bryan's ham sandwich in front of him. "My partner's bringing your drink," she said, and she walked over to a large table where four other deputies were already eating. Apparently the protocol for the fuzz was to eat together, not with the prisoners. Bryan scowled again.

"You want out, man?" the young car thief said quietly.

"What?" Bryan said.

"Ask the deputy to move the handcuff to your left wrist when he shows up with the drink. Tell him you eat and drink with your right hand. He'll likely switch it for you."

"What good will that do?"

The young punk grinned again. "Take a look down at the bottom of the table leg next to your left foot." He pointed with a jerk of his head.

Bryan hesitated a second and then did as he'd been instructed.

"I'll be damned!" he said quietly. The lag bolt at the bottom of this particular table leg was missing. The metal foot on the leg had a hole in it, but there was no bolt; not like the one to which his right wrist was attached.

"I reckon you can torque the table enough to get the handcuff under that leg."

Bryan looked up and saw young Deputy Harrison approaching with his tomato juice. He quickly covered the open bolt hole with his left shoe and said, "Any chance you could switch the cuffs to my left wrist, Deputy. My left hand is kinda useless, know what I mean? I do everything with my right."

The deputy put down the juice and his own plate of food and eyed Bryan briefly. "Yeah, I just bet you do," he said. "Hey, it's just a sandwich," he added dismissively. But he took a small key from his pocket and did exactly what Bryan had requested anyway. He didn't seem interested in what Bryan's left foot was covering. All these table legs were bolted to the floor; he knew that for sure.

"Thanks," Bryan said. "Enjoy your lunch."

Bryan waited a few seconds, until the deputy was some distance away, and then he said quietly, "Now what? Even if I can lift this side of the table enough to get myself loose, then what? There's armed deputies everywhere."

"You need a diversion, man. Listen, I'm done with my lunch, and so's my deputy." He pointed with his eyes this time, the left one not moving in exact concert with the other, both of them fluttering a little. "When he comes to get me, he'll take me out through that door, over there." He nodded to the doorway located at the far end of the room. "You see that pile of trays sittin' there, on the top of the trash container? Near the passageway to the restrooms. I'll pretend to slip on the floor over there and stumble into that pile, okay. I'll knock trays and dishes all over the place, make a hell-of-a-racket. That'll be when you take off. Out that door behind us." Again it was a jerk of the blonde haired head.

"Why the hell would you do this for me?" Bryan said.

Again the huge grin. "Why the hell wouldn't I?"

## Chapter Two

Arnold Towncraft stirred and moaned. It was still dark outside, and the rude awakening by the telephone ringing on his bedside angered him. He quickly grabbed the receiver, hoping the damned thing wouldn't wake Kathleen.

"Yeah," he said gruffly but as quietly as he could.

"Arnold, it's me. Frank."

"Good God, Frank. What the hell time is it?"

"It's breakfast time here, in Pittsburgh. In fact you probably can smell the onions in my omelet, and the bacon too, right?"

"Very funny, Frank." Arnold squinted at the alarm clock and could make out the glowing red numerals: 5:15. "Now that you've woken me up, and Kathleen, you may as well tell me what giant catastrophe compelled you to call me in the middle of the night.

These two old men loved each other dearly, but Arnold–who was actually Frank's nephew, though less than a decade separated them–was an impatient man and always cantankerous; especially first thing in the morning.

"That's just it, Arnold," Frank said. "This *is* catastrophic. Bryan escaped yesterday. Bryan Olmstead."

"What? You're kidding!" Arnold now sat bolt upright and unconsciously reached out a protective hand to touch his wife. If this was really happening... He dreaded the thought.

"No joke, Professor. He escaped from the courthouse yesterday around noon. Somewhere near San Diego. They were about to begin his competency hearing when he got away. Detective Segura called me a few minutes ago. You remember Art, right?"

"Of course. But he escaped from the courthouse? Don't they have armed guards in such places, Frank? My God, surely they'll find him pretty quick, won't they?"

Kathleen was now wide-awake and had become alarmed at what little she'd
heard. "What happened, honey?" she said. "What's going on?"

Arnold shook his head briefly and listened as Frank Dobson told all he knew about the escape of the deranged and highly dangerous serial killer and rapist, Bryan Olmstead. He and Frank, amateur detectives, had played a key role in getting Olmstead apprehended a few months prior. Frank was the real investigator of the two, having served as a police officer and then was a private eye for a long time, until he quit working, a few years ago. But Arnold had learned fast at the side of his uncle. A retired professor, he had become fascinated by crime and criminals after his own brush with murder charges years before. Together, they had solved Arnold's case and several others too; ones that had baffled the police completely. Both men loved these exciting and sometimes dangerous, always challenging, escapades, but this latest development now threatened their own personal security and that of some other people they had become fond of, like Brendan Carlson and his family. Brendan was the twin brother of the deranged killer. He had a different name from that of Bryan Olmstead because he had been adopted as a small child. Bryan had been raised by the twins' natural mother, and neither of the two boys had been aware of the existence of the other until they were in their forties. Then, by a quirky coincidence, they had literally locked psyches when Bryan began his killing spree in San Diego County, and it was the psychic connection between the two of them that had produced clues to the whereabouts of the killer twin and ultimately led to his arrest.

"Segura said he'd keep me posted, Arnold," Frank said. "But there's one other thing: "When Bryan was in the State Hospital, being evaluated, he obtained some newspaper articles about his arrest. He learned that it was his own brother who provided the keys to his arrest. He knows about you and me too, Segura is certain, and the roles we played in his apprehension."

Arnold climbed out of bed slowly and slipped his feet into leather slippers. It was not cold, being a typical summer morning in northern Oregon, but what he'd heard made him feel chilly. He struggled to don his robe while still holding the cordless phone. "Does Bryan know where his brother lives?" he asked anxiously. "Does he know where I live? Or you?"

"I don't know, Arnold, but we must start with the assumption that he can find out. As cruel and demented as this guy is he's also fiendishly clever, if you remember. We'd better assume the worst. You want to call Brendan and tell him?"

Arnold hesitated, not certain of the best thing to do. If Brendan knew, and if he told his wife, she would be a basket case until Bryan was recaptured. Surely the cops would find the bastard soon, and then there would be no problem. But if they didn't catch Bryan, and if Brendan didn't get adequate notice and a chance to protect his family... Arnold's head was filled with images of what Bryan might do in revenge. "Let me think about that for a bit, Frank," he said. "Any chance you could come out here? We might need you."

"We're supposed to be leaving tomorrow to go see Hilda's folks. They're in Cape Cod. Rented a cottage there for the summer months. It's been so damned hot here, we thought it would be nice to drive out to the coast and join them for a few days of–"

"It's not so hot here, Frank," Arnold said, interrupting, hoping perhaps unrealistically to persuade Frank to be by his side during what threatened to be an unnerving few days; maybe longer.

"I don't see how I can, Arnold. Hey, don't you worry. This guy had no money when he broke out and he has no friends that we know of. He'll have to lay low for a while until he can get his hands on some cash, for travel. If that's what he intends to do."

"But he's a criminal, Frank. He can and will steal money from any place! He could come up here seeking vengeance at any time. You know that!"

"It's possible, of course. But he could also skip south, to Mexico, and disappear forever. That's what I'd do."

"But Bryan Olmstead is a psychopath!"

"Yeah, I hear you. Hey, I'll call you again in a day or two, okay? Sooner if I hear anything new. Just try to relax. Everything'll work out just fine, you'll see."

"Oh, yeah? Then why the hell did you call me, you old coot?" Arnold said these words to himself, after returning the phone to its charging cradle

Despite Frank's attempt to make light of the new developments, Arnold felt extremely gloomy. Frank was always so damned positive, so upbeat, even when conveying bad news, and this was a really bad development. But that was one of the many reasons Arnold wanted him nearby at this time, to add protection, but also to lighten things up until the recapture of Olmstead. Arnold always felt comforted when Frank was around. Not just because he was an ex-cop, and carried a gun, but because... well, frankly he loved the guy!

While they dressed, and after, as they prepared breakfast together, Arnold and Kathleen shared their fears, their feelings, and they tried to decide whether or not to tell Brendan Carlson anything about his brother's escape from custody. They had not been married long, each for the second time. Kathleen having lost her first husband to a heart attack in his fifties, Arnold's wife dying of cancer after forty years of blissful marriage. Neither of them had children, so when they found each other they also found new reasons to feel young and vibrant again. They had purchased a lovely new home in The Dalles, a delightful bucolic community in Oregon, on the south side of the Columbia River Gorge. Arnold was on the Board of Trustees of his former employer, Biddlington College, located in Connecticut, and he also served on the board of three corporations. Independently wealthy from a bequest by his former father-in-law, and from his own shrewd investments, Arnold lived a life in elegant comfort with Kathleen, the former schoolteacher. Now, their comfort and maybe their lives were severely threatened, it seemed.

The Towncrafts ate breakfast that morning quietly, both feeling their apprehension grow. They talked a little about their young friends, the Brendan and Becky Carlson, and the two boys. Would Brendan's maniacal brother find them? This unspoken question, and all that it entailed, burned through both of them.

## Chapter Three

Brendan Carlson was a happy man, and he felt most fortunate. His beautiful wife, Rebecca–Becky, he called her–had been severely injured in an auto accident nearly two years ago. For many long months she had lingered near death in a deep coma and then, miraculously, she had suddenly recovered, suffered no permanent effects from her ordeal. In his desperate attempt to reach the unconscious Rebecca, Brendan had persuaded a professional psychologist to work with him, using hypnosis and other methodologies and Carl Jung's theory of a "collective" unconscious. At first this bizarre theory had seemed just that, a flight of fantasy. But soon after beginning the experiments–with Dr. Ruben Middlecoff, Arnold Towncraft's colleague and friend–instead of reaching the mind of his beloved and comatose Becky, Brendan had made some form of bizarre psychic contact with a serial killer. He witnessed, in his dreams and his hypnotic trances, the bestial acts of Bryan Olmstead; only later to realize this brutal killer was his own twin brother. He had not even been aware he had a brother at all, let alone a twin, so the shock of this, at the time, and what his genetic counterpart could do, was devastating.

Arnold Towncraft, along with his friend, Professor Ruben Middlecoff, and Frank Dobson, the ex-cop, had all come to Brendan's aid with moral support and direct help in bringing the murderous Bryan to justice. In the process, a deep friendship had developed between them all, but especially between Brendan and Arnold, though Arnold was older by more than a generation.

Rebecca's complete recovery was one reason Brendan felt fortunate, but another was the generosity of Arnold Towncraft. The old professor had paid a major part of Rebecca's outrageous medical expenses, but he had also used his connections to get Brendan a fresh start and a great new job in Oregon. So Brendan had moved his family up from San Diego County to the Portland area just a few weeks after Bryan's arrest. The young Carlson family loved their new environment, living in the hilly and picturesque countryside a few miles southeast of the city of Portland, where Brendan's office was situated. The Towncrafts' home was less than an hour away to the north.

At the same time Arnold and Kathleen Towncraft were ruminating about whether or not to tell Brendan the dreadful news about his brother's escape, Brendan was quietly dressing for his day at work. He loved his new job, and he arose each morning with boundless energy, anxious to take on all the new challenges that came with the territory. This particular morning, however, he felt a little less refreshed than usual. He'd had a disturbing dream about his brother, Bryan. He'd not thought much about Bryan for months, and had not dreamed of him since before the arrest. But last night... He stood looking in the mirror, adjusting his tie, trying hard not to think about Bryan, when he heard Rebecca stir and moan slightly.

"Hey," she said, "what in heaven's name were you dreaming about last night?"

He came to her side and sat on the edge of the bed, taking her hand in his.

"Morning, darling," he said, kissing her gently. "Sorry if I disturbed you."

"You were saying something incomprehensible, shouted a couple of times, and your legs were thrashing about like crazy."

"As Ebenezer Scrooge said, unsure of his Christmas Eve nightmare, 'It must have been the gravy.' But wait, we didn't have gravy with dinner last night, did we?"

Becky grinned. "We had spaghetti. Maybe it was my marinara sauce? But really, what were you dreaming about?"

Brendan reached under the bedclothes and gently squeezed her left breast. "I dunno," he lied. "But I love your sauce, if you get my drift."

"Come home for lunch," she said, still grinning wickedly, "and show me how much!"

"I'd love to, Hon, but I have meetings all day. I'll see you tonight, okay? I'll be as early as I can."

She smiled again and rolled over with a moan of pleasure. There was time to nap a little before waking their two boys, Tommy and Jason.

***

After they had eaten their breakfast, a simple concoction of cereals, fresh fruit and toast, served with some of Kathleen's famous gooseberry jam, the Towncrafts adjourned to their den with fresh coffee. Arnold used this small cozy room as his office, but the two of them often sat here in the morning, it caught the rising sun perfectly through the French doors. They would normally read the paper here, and talk of their plans for the day. But not this day. The newspaper lay on the coffee table, unopened.

"So what do you think we should do?" Arnold said.

"Brendan needs to know, Honey," Kathleen said. "He has a right to know."

"I suppose he does. Perhaps the police have already told him?"

"Do they know where he lives?"

"I honestly don't know that. I would have thought so. Surely they had some continuing contact with him after Bryan was incarcerated. Wouldn't you think? And they can track him down anyway, right?"

"They deliberately kept him out of the trial, if you remember. We were told they didn't need his testimony, or yours, and they didn't want Brendan to have the difficulty of facing his evil twin in court."

Arnold did remember... all too well. The fact that Brendan had envisioned some of his brother's vile acts, and had been able to track him down because of their psychic contacts, would have made challengeable evidence in any court proceedings. The prosecutors had decided to manage the case against Bryan without this kind of fantastic testimony from the brother of the accused.

Arnold looked at his watch. "Maybe I'll call him at his office in a few minutes. He gets an early start most days, I'm told."

Towncraft was a major shareholder in the firm Bryan Carlson worked for as General Sales Manager. The CEO of the company was a close friend of Arnold and had hired Brendan on the professor's recommendation.

"He doesn't have to tell Becky if he doesn't want to, right?" Towncraft continued, still very unsure about what he had decided to do, and still feeling remarkably edgy. "That will be his choice to make."

"Oh, I'd want to know, if it were me," Kathleen said, and Arnold knew she was right.

"You were going to go into Portland today, weren't you?" he said. "The Republican women's luncheon. That is today, right?"

"Yes, but I think I'll cancel. I feel quite unnerved."

They were seated side-by-side on a small loveseat, and Arnold reached out and placed his arm across Kathleen's shoulder, attempting to comfort her. "I'll go with you if you want. There's some shopping I should do. I need a new blazer for our cruise, and my tux needs cleaning."

Kathleen smiled at her husband. They had first met on a cruise ship and they were planning another cruise to Alaska in a few weeks. This would be their third sailing together.

"That's very nice of you, sweetheart," she said, "but don't you think you should hang around here, just in case... you know."

"Well, as Frank said, there will probably be no new developments to worry about for a couple of days." He paused. "But, you know, Bryan could have stolen a car last night and be halfway here by now."

"Oh, my dear Lord!" Kathleen said, placing her hand over the lower part of her face, so scared she almost spilled her coffee. "Do you really think so?"

Arnold wished he'd been more careful with his choice of words. "Well, that would be possible, I suppose. But it's not likely. Look, let's both go to Portland. I have to see our attorney on some tax issues, and I really do need a new blazer. I also want to find you something special."

Kathleen smiled again. As crusty and unemotional as her husband was, much of the time, he was romantic. He never made generous gifts on special occasions, but he often managed to find something unique to do at other times, for no particular reason, an exceptional gift for her as a surprise. She loved Arnold dearly, which had surprised her completely at first, following the loss of her beloved first husband. These gestures of generosity by Arnold were mere icing on the cake of their special relationship.

## Chapter Four

Marge Winters was thinking of closing up shop when he came in, the simple little door bell on a flat metal spring chirping his arrival. He looked familiar, somehow, this potential customer. But she couldn't quite place him.

"Good afternoon, sir?" Marge said cheerfully.

"I'll just browse, if that's all right," the man said.

"Go right ahead," she said. "Prices are on the bottom of most items, but I'll be right here if you have questions."

Marge and her sister ran a small gift shop and art gallery called "Two Sisters," in the village of Julian, California, a hamlet set high in the hills some forty miles east of San Diego. Julian is filled with tourists in the summertime, but at this time of day, and at this altitude, it was a bit chilly, so most casual visitors to the village had headed down the hill already. Marge would usually close up her gift shop by five in the afternoon, but this latecomer was the only customer she'd seen since lunchtime, so she gladly waited to see if he would purchase something. He really didn't look like the artsy type, she thought, but one never knew. Sometimes looks can be deceiving.

"Is Elaine here, Marge?" the man said, now in the far corner of the shop, looking out the side window, into the street.

This question startled Marge, and she hesitated for a moment, detecting a note of familiarity in the voice of the man. "You know my sister?" she said, overlooking the fact that the man obviously knew her own name too. She nervously eased around the end of the small glass-topped showcase she used as a counter, hoping to get another look at this customer.

He suddenly appeared before her, emerging from behind the antique room divider on which were displayed the work of some local artists. Grinning, he moved quickly to the store entrance, turned over the sign so that it would read "CLOSED" on the outside, bolted the door and said, "Surely you remember me, Marge. John Norton. Come on! I was your tenant; remember? I rented your upstairs room for a while. It's not that many months ago."

Suddenly she did remember. "Oh, my God!" she gasped. "But I thought you were in the..."

He thrust his face so close she could smell his breath as he said, "In prison?" His eyes were wide as saucers, and he smiled falsely. "Oh, yeah, I was in jail, Marge. But, as you can see, I am now a free man. Surprise!"

"What... What are you doing here? What do you want with me?"

John Norton smiled even more broadly as he came closer. It was a vicious smile, and Marge knew that this man's name was not really John Norton; it was Bryan Olmstead. She also knew what he had come for.

## Chapter Five

Detective Segura had just opened up his lunch when the call came to his desk phone. He cursed and picked up the handset, "Segura," he said gruffly.

"I got bad news for you, Art."

Segura recognized the voice immediately. It was his friend and former colleague, John Borden, now in the main office of the San Diego County Sheriff's department, in the City of San Diego itself. Segura was attached to the Vista substation.

"I'm eating, John. I don't take bad news until I'm finished. The only time you ever call these days, it seems, it's always bad news. So what's up? You got erectile dysfunction again? That it?"

"Very funny, my friend. But you'll not be so full of humor when you hear what happened."

"It's old news, John. I heard it last night. I got connections down there, where all you guys polish your brown noses with Kiwi, remember? You're talking about Olmstead, right?"

"I don't mean the escape, Art. That *is* old news. But the son-of-a-bitch killed two women last night, up in Julian. Two

27

women who run a gift store up there. He found his way to Julian by–"

"Not Marge Winters and her sister?"

"Yeah. The same. Olmstead rented a room from them just before he was caught, last fall, you'll remember. He evidently found out they played a small part in his arrest. Used a knife this time, not a gun, like before. Stuck 'em both the same way. Sliced them up like you wouldn't believe."

Segura groaned and went silent. Bryan Olmstead had evidently become something even more vile and treacherous than a murderous sexual predator. Now, he was an animal on the rampage, seeking revenge. God only knew who would be his next target. Hell, the Winters sisters didn't do that much to help the police...

"You still there, Art?" Borden said.

"Yeah, I'm here. This is one of those times when I wish I was a bank clerk or something. But I'm here, John, and like you, I sometimes get exposed to the handiwork of some of the world's worst animals. Man, oh, man." Segura paused. "Hey, how do you know it was Olmstead, anyway?"

"He left a note, saying, 'My blood brother, Brendan, knows exactly why,' and at the bottom he added. 'Catch me if you can, Pigs!' Brendan Carlson is the brother, right? What d'you suppose that part meant?"

"He probably blames his brother for being captured, and rightly so. But he might also blame his brother for the lousy childhood he had, since Brendan's had a much better life, and then some! Bryan's a total psycho, you know."

"He sure as hell is. But as fucked up as he is, he seems to be able to get around real well. He escaped shortly after noon and by three he'd found a car or a truck and by five last night he'd killed these two women in Julian. God knows where he'll go next."

"Oh, man! You're right, of course. We have to find the son-of-a-bitch. Any suggestions on where we go from here?"

"You really ought to warn everyone who might possibly be a target for Olmstead, Art. If he's on the rampage, seeking revenge, as now seems the case, a number of people could be at risk. We'll contact the police in each area if you give us a list of where they all live. We know some of the names, but you probably know more."

"I already called Frank Dobson, John, soon as I heard of Olmstead's escape. You remember Frank, right? The old retired Pittsburgh cop. Sharp old coot. He said he'd alert the Towncrafts and the Carlsons. They're all up in Oregon, so they may be out of danger. You never know, though. Any clue as to which way Olmstead was headed when he left Julian?"

"No, he didn't add that little detail to his note. Anyway, Bert Sampson asked me to help you on this the case in any way I can. Considering you made the original arrest, you should–"

"Good old Bert? I thought he was ready for retirement. Say, John, how in God's name did this bastard get loose? He was at the courthouse, for Christ's sake!"

"Yeah. Crazy, right? We were all threatened with silence on this one, Art, so I'll not tell you that sorry story over the phone. Ever since Richard Tuite's escape, a couple of years back, the Sheriff's been angry as a cornered badger. But what I want to know is how the hell you found out? We're still holding back everything, here, even from the media."

"Like I said, I've got connections. Listen, there's Olmstead's natural mother to worry about, she lives somewhere in Arizona these days, I have no idea exactly where. Sarah is her first name. The shrinks are all convinced he was abused by her, said he had a hatred for her like a snake hates a mongoose. Other than that, I– Oh, I suppose the close friends of Brendan Carlson and his wife–the Batholomes, Tim and Trish. They should be put on the alert. They didn't move to Oregon, so they are still in the same home as before, in Rancho Bernardo, right next door to where the Carlsons used to live. And they have a teenage girl. Man, this animal might just see her as– Listen, I'll handle all these folks, okay."

***

As Brendan Carlson was driving home, after a long day at work, he started to reflect on the dream he'd experienced the previous night. He had not felt as deeply involved in this dream, not like before. This time he knew who the featured person was, the person inside whose skin he seemed to be doing the bestial acts. In this latest dream he saw himself killing two women whose faces were obscured. These were not young, lithe and attractive women, as had been his brother's victims before his arrest, but their plump middle-aged bodies were butchered unmercifully, just the same, just as horrifically. Brendan couldn't begin to explain the sense of detachment he felt in this particular dream. The faces of the victims were blurred, and the experience, while disturbing, was not utterly soul-destroying, as his first experiences had been, before he knew what was happening to him. He was consoled by the fact that Bryan was in jail, now, about to be evaluated for competency to stand trial for the brutal slaying and rape of three young women, so he knew this could not be his brother up to his old tricks again. God, it had taken a hellish long time to get this case ready for trial!

*So what did this latest dream mean?* Brendan realized he was tired and extraordinarily tense, working hard to build confidence in his new job. Maybe that was it, nothing more sinister. Or maybe it was some kind of psychological flashback? He surely didn't want or need to make psychic contact with his brother again, even if Bryan was safely in jail. He glanced at the dashboard clock, realizing he was running a little later than he'd told Becky he'd be. Pushing the button that enabled his hands-free cell phone, he sighed deeply, hoping Becky wouldn't be too upset.

"On Star Ready," the mechanical voice said.

"Call Home," Brendan said, still marveling at this technology in his Cadillac.

It was Tommy who answered, after just two rings.

"Hey, Kiddo," Brendan said to his youngest son. "What's up?"

"Mom says you're late, Dad."

"Yeah, I am. Is she mad?"

"Nope, not really. But she fed us already, kept yours and hers hot. It's meat loaf."

"Yummy. Let me talk to her, will you."

"Hi, Bren," Becky said, showing no animosity in her voice. "I fed the boys. Hope you don't mind. Where are you?"

"I'll be there in a few minutes. Sorry I'm late. A busy day. You mad at me?"

"No, not really. I know you're in love with your new job, so I'm a little jealous is all. But drive carefully, and I'll have a glass of that new Cabernet ready when you get here. Oh, I almost forgot. Tim called. He wants you to call him back as soon as you can. Says it's urgent. Wouldn't tell me what it's all about."

"Okay, I'll call him from the car. See you in ten minutes or so."

Brendan hadn't spoken to Tim Bartholome in weeks. It seemed odd, not living next door to his oldest and best friend and Trish, Tim's lovely wife, Trish. They had for several years been next-door neighbors in Rancho Bernardo. The four close friends had wept openly when Brendan and Rebecca left, heading more than a thousand miles north, and they had promised to call each other often. But Brendan had become so involved in his new job, Rebecca in setting up their new home, that, well… such promises often get broken despite good intentions. Brendan pushed the phone button on his steering wheel again as he took the exit off Highway 26 onto the road that led to his hilltop house. The sun had set several minutes earlier, but there was still a beautiful pink glow on the snow-covered Mount Hood, looming large to his left in the darkening sky.

"Hi, Tim, it's me. What's up?"

"Oh, Bren, thank goodness you called. Are you at home?"

Tim's voice sounded strained, so Brendan knew something was amiss. "No, I'm in the car? Why? What is it? Is it Mom?"

Brendan had tried hard to persuade his mother to move to Oregon with them, but she had resisted, saying she had friends all over San Diego county, people she would miss terribly. Brendan knew this excuse had been fake–his mother's friends were few in number–but he also knew how hard it would be for his adoptive mother to uproot after all the years she'd spent in the San Diego area. He and Becky had deliberately bought a home large enough for Emily Carlson to be comfortable, in case she changed her mind, but so far she still she resisted.

"Bryan escaped, Bren."

"What? Holy shit! When? How?"

"I don't know the details. Sometime yesterday he took off. But here's the worst part. Remember Marge Winters and her sister? They had that little gift store up in Julian. Eileen; was that the sister's name?"

"Elaine. What about them?"

"Well, after Bryan escaped he made his way up the mountain and killed both of them. Happened last night. They were found first thing this morning. He used a knife on them."

Brendan almost drove off the road as he heard these words, and he instantly realized the significance of his dream. Once again, in the height of Bryan's bestial activities, Brendan had made psychic contact with his twin brother. Would it happen again? Was he destined to suffer more of these awful visions and dreams, as he had before?

"Oh, my God. NO!" Brendan thumped the steering wheel with the heel of his hand.

"I know how you feel, pal. Sorry I had to be the one to... you know."

There was a lengthy silence between the two men. Eventually, Brendan said quietly, "Have you told Trish?"

"No, I haven't. Just heard not long ago. She's out right now, with Marlie. I suppose I'll have to tell them both sometime soon. What about the Towncrafts? Will you tell them?" Marlie was Tim and Trish's teenage daughter.

"Yeah, I suppose I have to. They could be at risk, too, right?"

"Detective Segura said everyone who knows you could be at risk. This guy's a maniac, so you just can't tell what he'll do next, or where he'll go."

"Do me a favor, will you, Tim. Call my mother right away. Make sure she's okay. You have her number, right?"

"Yeah. No problem. Segura said she was being protected, but I'll call her anyway. Should I tell her what's going on?"

Brendan hesitated a few seconds. Finally, he said, "She'll hear it soon enough anyway, so yeah, tell her about the escape. Don't say a word about the two women being killed, though. No sense scaring the hell out of her. Tell her I'll be in touch later this evening, okay?"

The two men agreed to remain in close contact over the next several days and each disconnected their phone. Brendan was deeply concerned as he pulled into his driveway. *What would he tell Becky?*

## Chapter Six

Dave Sargent was not usually still awake at this time each night, but tonight he was still up and alert. Not that his life had suddenly become meaningful, filled with exciting things to do, or in fact anything to do, but something unusual had happened,

More often than not Dave fell asleep on his living room couch soon after dinner. He would typically drink a beer or two, watch a few sitcoms on the television and then doze off. Several hours later, depending on the number of beers consumed, he'd stir again and stagger off to bed. His lonely life didn't vary much. The trailer park in which he lived was restricted to seniors, so it was a quiet place. He liked it that way. Dave, like many of his neighbors, was actually waiting to die, not having any particular reason to live. His wife had been gone for eleven years and his two sons he never heard from. They didn't care about him at all, apparently.

This evening, however, Dave had been unusually daring. He had invited his next-door neighbor in for pizza and a beer. Sarah Olmstead had lived in the mobile home next to Dave Sargent's place for a little less than two months. They had exchanged greetings a few times, but nothing more. He knew she was a renter, not an owner, so he guessed she'd not remain long; they seldom did. Earlier this day, he had seen her planting pansies in the window boxes that made her trailer seem a little more like a house than most of the crappy places in this run-down park, and he'd taken the opportunity to chat with her. Then, because she seemed friendly enough, he'd suggested she drop by later and share a home-delivery pizza. He was more than a little surprised that she'd said yes.

So they had watched a bad movie together on the television and shared a few beers. Each of them had also told some bare details of their life before becoming old and forgotten. Dave learned that Sarah had one son, living in California someplace, but she had no other family. "He called me just yesterday," she'd said with a small show of something like pride. "I had no idea he knew my number, but he found it somehow. Told me he'd drop by one of these days and asked how to find this place." Sarah smiled a little as she said this, so Dave assumed she had a good relationship with her son.

Dave himself told of his former wife and two sons, but he didn't mention that he had no idea where the two boys lived or what they did for a living. All things considered, the evening had been a refreshing change for Dave, and it was eleven-thirty before he even noticed the time. Sarah said, "Time flies when you're having fun," and Dave took this as a sign maybe they would do it again, or perhaps something even more intimate? He wasn't sure he could handle such a get-together, but he would cross that bridge if he came to it. It had been such a long time since he'd spent time with a woman; any woman.

After saying goodnight to Sarah, Dave sat and watched a late-night news show for a few minutes, on a Phoenix affiliate station of NBC. Phoenix was the nearest large city to the Arizona town of Kingman, where this run-down trailer park housed some eighty-five senior citizens in fifty-odd variously decrepit but uniformly unattractive mobile homes. He'd opened another beer, though he knew he'd regret it. His highly enlarged prostate would keep him up all night at the best of times. He was about ready to take the half-finished can of beer to his bedroom when he heard the noise. It sounded somewhat like a muffled scream, or maybe it was a loud sneeze. It came from next door, it seemed certain, from Sarah Olmstead's trailer. He waited to see if there would be other noises, his anxiety level climbing a little. Hearing nothing further, he went to the front window and pulled aside the dusty curtains. There were dull street lamps spaced every forty yards or so, but none close by. However, in the dim light Dave saw the shadowy figure of a man leave the front of Sarah's home and stroll to the footpath that led to the visitor's parking lot, located beyond the homes across the road. Then, he saw headlights of a vehicle flash between the trailers across from his. Someone had evidently visited Sarah and then left; but she had been home less than forty minutes, so how could that be? Was it any of his business? Dave hesitated, wondering if he should go next door and check on his new friend, see if she was all right. He could call her, he thought, but he didn't have her number. He could maybe persuade grumpy old Dan Watson to give him Sarah's number. Dan managed the park, or at least collected the lot rental for the absentee owner. No, Sarah might think he was after something if he knocked at her door, so that option seemed unwise. Anyway, it was too late to call Watson. Dave crossed the room and turned off the television and the lights. Out the window of his tiny kitchen he could see the glow of lights coming from Sarah's trailer, but he could see nothing except that there were lights on in her living room. It was silent.

Dave decided he should go to bed, and to hell with it. The man who had left Sarah's house had not seemed in a particular hurry, not like a criminal would, so why should he suspect anything bad had happened? There had been just the one sound, and maybe it was not a scream at all. Yeah, it must have been a sneeze. He picked up his beer and took it to the tiny bedroom, determined he would check on Sarah in the morning, just to be sure.

Two hours later, his bladder throbbing, Dave stirred and made his way to the bathroom to relieve himself. As he stood at the toilet, dribbling in customary fashion despite the intensity of his need, he became aware that the light from his neighbor's living room was still illuminating parts of his own home. He finished urinating, or nearly so, and wandered to the kitchen window again. He still could see nothing through the window of Sarah's trailer except that the same lights were still on. Though he was still in his pajama bottoms, the way he always slept, he decided he should go outside to investigate. Perhaps he would be able to see something through the window if he got closer.

Because there was a rickety trellis supporting unhealthy-looking dog rose brambles and spanning most of the gap between the two houses, near the front, Dave went to his back door.

Outside, he found it a little cold and he wished he'd put on a sweater. But he quickly made his way along the narrow space between the trailers, brushing the spider webs off his face, and he peered into Sarah's living room window. Other than the fact that the lights were on, he saw nothing. Wait! There was a dark stain on the badly worn green carpet, it looked like gravy or something such, but it was partly obscured by the end of Sarah's tan vinyl sofa. Could it be blood? It looked more brownish than red, but Dave supposed it really could be blood? So now what should he do? Nah, it was probably gravy, or maybe an old wine stain. He walked to Sarah's back door, located on the far side of her trailer, and he gently tried the handle. It was locked.

The passageway on this side of Sarah's mobile home was open all the way to the street, so Dave took that route, intent on trying the front door. Halfway there, however, he stumbled into a trashcan, causing one hell of a clatter. A dog barked in protest, and yet Dave knew no one in the immediate vicinity had a dog. Not on this street. Maybe it was a stray? They often saw stray dogs and other animals in this park, the fence being in such bad shape. No dog showed up, however, and the barking soon stopped, so Dave groped his way forward, now more cautious. Surely Sarah would have been awakened by the noise he'd made, if she were alive? He hated himself for what he was now thinking.

"Sarah, are you all right?" Dave said, half whispering, but he also knocked firmly on the door.

He knocked again, but still no answer.

He was now quite concerned. He supposed that Sarah might use sleeping pills of some sort, but what if she had really been attacked by the shadowy figure he had seen crossing the street earlier? He went back the way he had come, testing each of the windows along the way. A couple were open a crack, but they had some kind of device to prevent them being opened fully, so he wasn't able to get inside. He was not sure he could have hoisted himself up high enough anyway. He called Sarah's name into each of the partly open windows, but didn't dare raise his voice too high. Old Mrs. Giddings would bitch for a week if anyone made noise at night. Joan Giddings was Sarah's neighbor on the other side.

Giving up, Dave retraced his steps, this time managing to avoid the trashcan, and he was soon back inside his own home, feeling perplexed and quite chilled. He looked at the clock on his kitchen wall. It was now 2:17 a.m., far too late to think of calling Dan Watson or anyone else, so Dave opened up another beer, the last one he had, and he went back to his lumpy bed. He didn't sleep well, however, and the rest of the night seemed to go so slowly he thought he'd never see the light of day.

Finally the morning did come, and at 6:25 a.m. Dave arose and took a shower. As he dressed himself he reflected on the middle-of-the night mystery over his neighbor, and he came to the conclusion that he would simply knock at Sarah's door again; but not until after he'd had breakfast. As he placed the cooking fat in his frying pan, and cracked two eggs, he couldn't help glancing out his kitchen window, hoping to see signs of life next door. All still seemed silent.

40

\*\*\*

"Aaaaagh!"

The scream of apparent anguish from her husband scared Rebecca Carlson. He had dozed on the couch, after dinner, and Rebecca had let him sleep. She had been contemplating attempts to wake him as she watched a late-night talk show on television. She rushed to Brendan's side immediately, even though she knew he was merely dreaming. She had seen his slumped body twitch several times before, and he had mumbled something incoherent.

"It's okay, honey," she said, taking his hand in hers. "You were dreaming again, weren't you?"

Brendan looked at her with a dazed expression, confused and more than a little alarmed. "Jesus!" he said. "That was awful." He sat up and rubbed his eyes.

"You're dog-tired, honey. Working too hard, no doubt. Come on, let's get to bed. It's getting late. Take a hot bath why don't you? I'll bring you a little brandy."

Brendan remained unsettled, but he knew the suggestion Becky had made was a sensible one. He had to be up and at it early the next day, so sleep seemed attractive, but he was not anxious to experience the same dream again. He slowly roused himself and made his way upstairs. Minutes later, reclining in a nearly full bathtub, steam swirling everywhere, he took the brandy from his wife and downed most of it in a single gulp.

"Like me to scrub your back?" she said, kneeling beside the tub.

"Yeah," he replied, "that sounds great." He reached for the sponge.

41

As Rebecca soaped and rubbed his back, Brendan began to describe his dream. She knew he would.

"This was as bad as any I experienced before," he said. "You know, while you were unconscious. This time, though, the victim was an older woman. I felt myself stabbing her in the belly, several times. It was awful, Beck, and the detail... Listen, I have to tell you something. Something very alarming, okay?"

Rebecca stopped scrubbing and stared hard at him. "You're scaring me, Bren," she said quietly, her eyes wide in anticipation. She placed her soapy hand over the lower part of her face and shook her head. "I knew you had something serious on your mind when you got home. You hardly said a word over dinner, not even to the boys."

"I'm sorry," he said. "I really am, but I learned something from Tim. My brother escaped the day before yesterday. I don't know the details, but my dreams have me convinced that... that he's killing people again. I just feel it. Last time, the victims were always strangers, to him, but this time, I–"

The dreadful look on her husband's face frightened Rebecca even more than the words he spoke, and she reached out for him at once, stifling his words as she pressed his face to her breast. "Hush," she whispered. "Don't say any more. Not now. Don't even think it, okay?" She eased back and kissed him gently, tears now trickling down her face.

Brendan had told Rebecca all about the awful dreams and visions he'd experienced when his twin brother had been abducting, raping and ultimately killing a series of young women. This had occurred while Rebecca was in a coma, after a nearly fatal auto crash, and it had been all the more disturbing because, at the time, Brendan had not even known of the existence of his twin brother.

Separated from his twin in the adoption of Brendan by a loving childless couple named Carlson, Bryan Olmstead had been raised without being told of his brother's existence. The infant Brendan Olmstead became Brendan Carlson, and he grew up to be a productive member of society, a loving husband and father of two boys himself. He too did not know of his brother.

Bryan was physically, sexually and psychologically abused by his natural mother, Sarah, and her live-in boyfriend, from a very early age, and he became a problem child, a delinquent teen and eventually a psychotic rapist and killer. Many years later, in some bizarre way, Brendan had made psychic contact with this unknown evil twin, his channeled visions terrorizing him at the time, but eventually what he saw in these bizarre contacts had led to the apprehension of Bryan, the killer. The dreams and awful experiences of their psychic connection ceased while Bryan was in prison, but now Brendan had apparently made contact again. Unconscious, unwilling, deeply disturbing contact. It had started the very same day Bryan escaped.

"I... Becky, this time the woman I killed... or rather, Bryan killed... she was his mother. My mother. He killed two innocent women, in Julian, and now he has killed our mother."

Rebecca still held Brendan's face in her hands. He looked almost lifeless all of a sudden, his realization seeming to sap his energy in some awful way. The fear in his eyes was gone, but it

43

was replaced by a pall, a totally void expression that scared Becky, chilled her completely. Never had she seen him so sad, so utterly defeated.

"But you've never met your natural mother, Bren. Never even seen a photo, have you?"

"No, I haven't," he said. "But I know it was her." He glanced at his wife briefly, and then he looked down into the soapsuds that surrounded him and he began to sob. At that moment the telephone rang, startling Rebecca but seeming not to impact Brendan at all. Hesitating for a moment, considering just allowing the message machine to take the call, it being so late, Rebecca finally went to the bedroom and picked up the phone by their bedside.

"Hello," she said, as calmly as she could, despite her emotional state, "This is Rebecca Carlson."

"Becky, it's Arnold Towncraft. Sorry to call you so late, but I have some important information for Brendan. Is he there?"

"He's taking a bath, Arnold. Is this about Bryan's escape?"

"You know?"

"Brendan learned it from Tim earlier today. Oh, Arnold, this is such dreadful news, but surely the police will–"

Rebecca was interrupted by Brendan, who now stood behind her with a towel wrapped around his lower body. "Let me talk to him, Hon," he said.

"Here's Brendan, Arnold" Rebecca said into the phone. "He just climbed out of the tub."

44

Brendan thanked Arnold for the call and quickly told of his renewed visions and dreams. He also revealed his conviction about Bryan's latest victim.

"I guess we'll just have to wait and see," Towncraft said, obviously shaken. "I doubt if that would surprise the police though. Listen, I'm sorry I didn't call you sooner. We found out yesterday morning, from Frank, but I couldn't make up my mind about whether or not to tell you at all. There may be no reason to worry, but on the other hand I felt sure you'd... Anyway, after thinking about it, I decided to bring you the bad news. You had a right to know."

"Thanks, Arnold. I should have known right away, without being told. I had this very bad dream last night. I should have known."

"You saw him again? Like last time?"

"Yeah. Pretty much the same. Have you told Kathy about his escape?"

"She knows. I asked Frank to come out here to help us, but he's gone to Cape Cod for a few days. How about Middlecoff? You want his help? The dreams and such, you know."

Brendan paused. Middlecoff was the psychologist who had helped him deal with his awful dreams the last time, when he was also deeply depressed about Rebecca's condition, and he'd found it helpful. But did he need him now? He wasn't sure.

"I don't think so, Arnold. I may give him a call in a day or two, but this time around at least I know exactly what's going on and who it is I'm channeling. Last time, I was... well, you remember what it was like last time."

"Yes, I sure do. Listen, try to get a decent night's sleep, if you can. I'll see what else I can find out first thing in the morning and I'll get back to you as soon as possible."

But Brendan had no intention of going to bed right away. Not now. He realized he needed to check on his mother, his adoptive mother, Emily Carlson. Based on the latest horrendous developments and his certainty that Bryan was on a killing spree again, he needed to know Emily was safe. But she would be asleep by now, wouldn't she? Dilemma: wake her up unnecessarily, or risk leaving it until the morning? He chose the latter of these options, but in doing so he condemned himself to a night of poor sleep, worrying. But then again, if he had fallen deeply asleep, no telling what dreams would invade his unconscious mind, what demons would haunt him again.

***

The mid-morning call to Art Segura's home didn't exactly come as a surprise, but what Art heard from an Arizona State civilian employee still managed to shock the experienced detective deeply.

"Detective Segura, this is Jake Condis of the Arizona Department of Public Safety. I'm told you're the one who originally arrested Bryan Olmstead. Is that right?"

"Yeah, that would be me. Public Safety, did you say?"

"Yes, sir. The Mohave County Sheriff called us into a local homicide case because they suspected it might involve someone already in the criminal justice system in California."

"Olmstead escaped prison just two days ago. Maybe you knew that?"

"Yes, we learned that from the San Diego Sheriff's office this morning. They also gave me your name and number. Got bad news, Detective. Olmstead's mother was killed last night, in her mobile home near Kingman. Multiple knife wounds."

"Oh, my God!"

"Yeah, my sentiments exactly. Did you ever meet Sarah Olmstead?"

"No, I never did. Never even spoke with her. Not a model mother, by all accounts, but she didn't deserve to die. Not like this. Any indication that her son did it?"

"Nothing concrete. The man who found her was an acquaintance, says Sarah told him she'd heard from her son just the day before. Bryan called and asked for directions to her house, apparently, and he said he would visit soon. Other than that–"

"The son-of-a-bitch did it! I just know he did. No weapon found? Fingerprints? Other evidence?"

"The crime scene unit is still working on it, so it'll be a couple of days before we know much. I'll FAX you a copy of their report when they're done. Vista office, right?"

"Yeah. I'm at home right now, Jake. I had one of those all-nighters; know what I mean? Spent hours yesterday trying to track down Sarah Olmstead, as a matter of fact. Guess I didn't make it in time, did I? And now–"

"Don't blame yourself, Art. She has moved three times in the last few months, apparently. But listen, if this really was her son he may have other targets on his list. I learned quite a bit about Bryan Olmstead from your friend, John Borden. This is one bad dude, and he appears bent on revenge."

"You got that right. He didn't leave a note this time?"

"What?"

"Last time, he left a note. Mentioned his twin brother's name."

"No, nothing like that."

"Maybe it wasn't Bryan. On the other hand– Listen, keep me posted will you. This whole damned mess seems to be headed to hell in a hand basket, and you're right. I got work to do."

When Segura hung up he sat for a while at the cheap chrome dinette in his kitchen, and he drank a huge mug of muddy coffee, barely warm. His system needed caffeine, lots of it, so he didn't care how bad it tasted. He lived alone, had for several years, and at this moment he felt especially melancholy. He knew he was in for a hell of a day, perhaps many days.

After a few minutes in deep thought, Segura touched base with his boss, Lieutenant Jack Jones, who he regarded with disdain and who everybody kidded about his name. "Sing us the Love Boat theme, Jack," everybody used to say to his face, referring to the famous singer/namesake. Behind his back they said different things about the lieutenant: less humorous, more critical. "He's a bloody bureaucrat of the first order," Segura would often say to anyone who would listen. He filled Jones in with the bare details of what he knew and asked if the CSI team had come up with anything of value at the scene where Marge and Elaine Winters were murdered.

"What's to find?" the lieutenant said harshly into the phone, and Segura heard the squeak of Jones' chair. He hated that sound. "We know it was Olmstead, Art, he left a damned note."

"Well, now, let me see... I'll play at being a detective for a second. Hey, what if someone saw Olmstead while he was in Julian? What if he had taken a disguise, a fake beard, a red wig, something like that? Or maybe somebody got a make on his vehicle. Surely that would be of some help, don't you think, Lieutenant?"

"Don't be a smart ass, Art. Just get busy and make sure no one else gets killed in this damned spree, you hear me? I'll get Johnson to follow up with the CSI team and let you know. You comin' in here today or not?"

Art was sleep-deprived, too depressed, too discouraged, so he knew he'd better not say what he wanted to. Instead, he growled, "I'll be there sometime this afternoon. Right now I'm going to go see Tim Bartholome, make him a little more aware of what risks he and his family faces. I'd also like to talk Brendan Carlson's mother into taking a trip up to Oregon, visit with her son. She's a nice lady, wouldn't want anything nasty to happen to her, would we."

Ten minutes later, Segura was at the offices of Vestramed, Inc., the firm where Tim Bartholome worked as a marketing executive. Tim was in a management meeting, he was told, but Segura was able to persuade Tim's secretary to interrupt and bring him to the lobby. Segura requested they go outside, into the parking lot.

"What's going on, Lieutenant?" Tim asked anxiously. "God, it's hot out here."

"I'm just a Sergeant, but thanks anyway. I'm here to bring you up to date, Mr. Bartholome. But I also think it would be wise for you to take your family off somewhere for a vacation, someplace away from your home, just for a few days, maybe a week."

"But I can't just– What the heck is going on? I take it you haven't caught Bryan Olmstead yet. Is that it?"

"That's right, sir, we haven't. And we have no idea where he is right now or where he's headed, but we do know he's on a killing spree. You and your family could be in danger. He–"

"No way. Why would he care about us?"

Segura took a step closer to Tim and said quietly, despite his frayed patience, "Listen, he killed his own mother last night, in Arizona. He gets around pretty readily, so you really ought to take your wife and daughter off to someplace safe. Understand what I'm saying?"

"Can't you provide protection for us? Isn't that what the police is supposed to do?"

Segura glared hard at Tim. "Ordinarily, yes. But we don't have the resources to provide round-the-clock protection for everyone who's a potential target for this bastard. The safest bet is for you to just get away. You've had no strange phone calls or anything like that, have you?"

"No, nothing like that. I suppose our daughter could have, but–"

"Where's your daughter right now?"

"Marlie? She's in school. You're not suggesting–" Tim was starting to feel more than a little threatened by the implications of this exchange. The detective seemed extraordinarily nervous himself. Was he just being cautious, or did he have some specific information he had not divulged?

"The only suggestion I'm making, Mr. Batholome, is that you get your wife and daughter, right now, and head off to some place without telling anyone where you're going. Contact me in a couple of days, I'll bring you up to date." He handed Tim a business card, which Tim pocketed without inspection.

"What about Emily Carlson, Brendan's mother? Are you suggesting the same thing for her?"

"As a single lady who lives alone and goes nowhere in particular every day, we're able to provide protection for her. But with you, both parents working and a child going to school every day, out with friends each evening if she's like most teenagers, that would be impossible. Anyway, I'm going to suggest to Mrs. Carlson that she go up and visit with Brendan, in Oregon."

Tim felt terribly uncertain about what to do. He had an important client coming in the following day, one he expected to sign a fat new contract worth several million dollars. Trish, a teacher, would rebel like crazy, he knew. She had mid-term exams coming up. As for Marlie, she was at the age where she rebelled at everything. She hated going off with her parents at any time. She would be especially problematical.

"I'll talk to my wife, see what she thinks. I do thank you for your concern and appreciate that you're–"

51

Segura stepped even closer to Tim and he squinted threateningly. "Look! This maniac is on a killing spree. You understand? You want to see pictures? Here!" He pulled from his jacket pocket several sheets of paper, folded and creased. He opened up the first of what Tim could tell were digital pictures, printed on ordinary copy paper in full color. The definition was not great, but good enough for Tim to see the body of a woman in a nightgown, her lower abdomen covered in blood from multiple stab wounds. Seeing this evidence of brutal mutilation, with all the blood, was supposed to be convincing; and it worked. Tim was shocked and horrified.

"Is this Bryan and Brendan's birth mother?" he asked, his voice hoarse from shock and tension.

"What's left of her," Segura said. "Want to see the pictures of Marge and Elaine Winters? They got similar treatment."

"No. Never mind. I get the message. Look, you've got work to do and so do I. Like you said, I'll be in touch. Maybe we'll drive up and spend a few days with Brendan and his–"

"Jesus H. Christ, no! That would be the worst thing you could do. And don't tell me where you're going, just go. Call me in two days. You got my number, there on the card. Office and cell. Here, let me give you my home number too, just in case."

Segura took a second business card from his wallet and quickly penciled another number on the back of it. He then turned and walked away, towards his car. After a few yards, he turned back and yelled, "Do not be tempted to tell even your boss where you're going, Mr. Bartholome. You hear me? You can tell him why, of course, but nothing more."

"It's a she, Detective."

"What?"

"My boss is a she."

"Yeah, yeah, whatever. That sorry day hasn't come for me, yet. But it will, I suppose. Christ! Seeya!"

Less than three hours later, Tim and Trish were waiting outside the year-round high school where their fourteen year-old daughter, Marlene, was in attendance. Or so they thought. But Marlie, as everyone called her, did not appear when all the other teenagers flooded out of the building at 2:45 p.m. and either ran for their cars, the school buses that lined up along the street, or stood around in groups gabbing. A small number of kids waited in frustration for a humiliating pick-up by a parent.

Marlie was a good student. Soon to be fifteen years old, she had skipped a grade, was now in the tenth, a full year younger than most tenth-graders. This was good news in one sense, and her parents were very proud of her, but it also meant that she was mixing with older kids, young men and women with raging hormones and an insatiable desire to be treated as adults. Marlie was easily led, Tim and Trish knew, and they were concerned about the peer influences she was experiencing.

They had briefly toyed with the idea of calling the school and getting Marlie yanked out of class early. Instead, they had gone home, thrown some of Marlie's things in a suitcase, packed bags of their own in a hurry and planned to surprise their daughter here, at school, grabbing her before she got on the bus for home.

Marlie had her own cell phone, but they knew the school required all such devices turned off while classes were in session. They tried calling soon after classes were supposed to end, but they found that Marlie's phone was not yet turned back on. That surprised them no end.

After hesitating for a couple of minutes, knowing that parents asking around for a fourteen or fifteen year-old was the kiss of death for any youngster, they decided to go inside and ask after her. Maybe she had an after-school assignment, or a meeting with a teacher. Marlie was not athletically inclined, so there was never a team practice. She played the flute and had band practice twice a week, but not today, a Tuesday. Just Mondays and Thursdays.

They had barely made it to the front steps of the main school building when Trish, who was now so antsy she could barely see straight, said, "Isn't that Janey over there, Tim? Look, there, talking to that tall boy in the red baseball cap."

Tim squinted, looking directly toward the afternoon sun. Janey was the daughter of their next-door neighbors, the ones who had purchased Brendan and Becky's house, and the girl had rapidly become one of Marlie's best friends. Yes, this certainly was Janey. Tim had often admired her blossoming figure, and he felt guilty doing so now.

"Sure is," he said, still amazed that a fifteen year-old girl could look so sexy. "C'mon, maybe she knows something."

"Hi, Mr. and Mrs. Bartholome," the pretty blond girl said, all smiles as they approached her.

"Do you have any idea where Marlie is, Janey?" Trish said, her anxiety all too evident.

"She left campus early today. Mr. Davidson had to go home, he was sick, so his last class was canceled. She and a few other kids went off to the mall. There were two guys with their own cars, and about ten of them piled in. They'll probably drop Marlie off at home, later."

Tim groaned. Being the parent of a teenager was bad enough at any time, but now, given what he was trying to accomplish and what the threats were, it was a nightmare.

"Thanks, Janey," he managed to say, relatively calmly. "Listen, if she contacts you, tell her to call me on my cell right away, will you. Something urgent has come up. Okay?"

"Sure. She'll probably call me soon. We're supposed to be going to a movie later." The smile she offered was dazzling.

Trish sighed deeply as they watched Janey and her friend run for a bus that was just about to pull away from the curb.

"Now what do we do?" she said, disconsolate.

Trish had experienced no difficulty getting permission to take off for a few days; that much had been a pleasant surprise for Tim. She had tenure, and she was highly regarded as an elementary school assistant principal. She had teaching duties, half-load, but there were plenty of substitutes available. She had her mid-term exams all prepared, so a sub could readily take over and proctor the tests for her. Tim had been a little surprised when she'd so willingly complied with his recommendation. He'd not even found it necessary to go into great detail about the women who had been so badly mutilated by the rampaging Bryan Olmstead.

"I guess all we can do is go home and wait for her to show up or call," Tim said. "We could go to the mall, I suppose, but chances are... Well, you know what it's like at the mall."

Not ten minutes later, as they were approaching their home, Tim's cell phone vibrated in his pocket. It was Marlie.

"What's up, Dad? Janey said to get you right away."

"Yeah, listen, Kiddo, you have to come home, pronto. Something urgent came up. I can't explain it on the phone, but we have to go away for a few days. All of us. We've packed some of your things and— Wait, better yet, just tell me exactly where you are and I'll come get you."

"Dad, I can't go anywhere. I've got plans. Me and Janey and a couple of other kids are going to a movie tonight. I thought we'd stay here at the Mall and grab a burger or something, for dinner, and then we'd just—"

"Marlie, I'm not asking you, I'm telling you. This is very important and it is actually a life-threatening thing, so don't give me any crap, okay."

"Dad, I'm not a little girl. I can't see why—"

"Marlie, there's a killer on the loose. For God's sake just do as I say."

"A killer? What would a killer want with me? With us? C'mon, Dad. Is Mom with you right now? Can I talk to her?"

Exasperated, Tim turned his phone over to Trish and was amazed at how strong she sounded: "Marlie, do exactly what your father said. You remember the killer Brendan Carlson helped get arrested, a year ago? Well, he broke out of jail and is on a wild killing spree again. The police think he could come after us next, so don't you give us any crap, young lady, just tell me where you are and wait right there for us. We'll be there in fifteen minutes. Got it?"

Even more amazing for Tim was that Trish's direct and forceful approach had worked. Marlie quietly told her mother where she could be picked up. Tim checked his rearview mirror and made a U-turn, heading back toward Rancho Bernardo's main indoor shopping complex. Though the late afternoon traffic was building, they soon had the grumpy Marlie safely in the car and were headed north.

Tim had made up his mind that a few days in Las Vegas would be a good idea, maybe even a pleasurable one despite the summer heat. Perhaps they would manage to scrape up some fun while they were there. But he didn't tell Trish or Marlie his plans, not until they were approaching the Nevada border, three hours later. By then Trish had guessed.

"Where are we going to stay?" she asked. "Bellagio?"

Tim grunted, knowing that even in the summertime Belagio's prices would be steep. "I thought we'd try to get a room at Ceasar's. With all the new places there, Ceasar's is a bargain these days. And they have that beautiful shopping complex...."

Trish smiled. She knew Tim was trying to appease her about having to leave on short notice. But she really was quite content on one level, though still inwardly alarmed about the reason for this trip.

Marlie was a lot less sanguine. She carefully checked her suitcase when they stopped at a gas station and was not happy with what she found, or rather what she did not find. She complained bitterly, whining about the favorite casual clothes that Trish had not packed. "And there's no swimsuit in here!"

Tim said, "I tell you what, ladies, can go shopping together when we get settled in Vegas. Buy anything you need, within reason."

Those were the magic words for Marlie, and she settled back into her seat quietly. She reached into her purse for her cell phone, but found that she could not get a signal. "Later," she muttered.

"You say something, sweetheart?" her mother said, sipping on the bottle of water she'd picked up at the gas station.

"Nah. Just talking to myself," Marlie said, vowing to try calling Janey again.

## Chapter Seven

The crunch of automobile tires on the driveway, followed by the thud of a car door and then the loud rap at their front door, all served to raise the anxiety level of the already shaken Arnold and Kathy Towncraft considerably. It was early in the morning, and they were not long out of bed, still in dressing gowns. Arnold glanced at Kathy anxiously and then at his wristwatch. The two days that had passed since hearing of Bryan Olmstead's escape had been some of the most distressing days of their lives, and they were scared.

"You suppose I should answer that?" Arnold said, feeling very unsure. But the lights were on inside the house and outside, in the driveway, so whoever was at the door would realize they were up and around.

"I wouldn't," Kathy said. "Ask them to identify–"

At that point they heard a voice from outside: "Arnold, it's me. Frank."

"Frank?" Arnold was suddenly relieved. "My goodness–"

He rushed to the door and opened it without hesitation. There stood his Uncle Frank in the early morning gloom, a large suitcase by his side.

"Sorry to scare you, Arnold," he said with a grin, "but I got in rather late last night, so I couldn't call you. Anyway, here I am."

"My God, what a surprise!" Arnold's pleasure quite evident. "Come in, Frank. Here, let me get your bag."

Kathy joined them in the expansive entry hall of the Towncrafts' gracious home
and the three of them embraced warmly.

"Your timing is impeccable, Frank," Kathy said. "I was just about to make breakfast. How would you like your eggs?"

Frank stipulated "Over, easy" and immediately excused himself, anxious to use the bathroom. Arnold took his suitcase up to the guest bedroom and when he returned he found Frank seated at the kitchen table, coffee in hand. Kathy was at work with frying pan and spatula.

"So what changed your mind, Frank?" Arnold said as he reached for the coffee pot himself. "Shouldn't you be in Cape Cod?"

Frank delayed his response, glancing briefly in Kathy's direction. He finally said, "I spoke with Art Segura late yesterday afternoon. He told me about Bryan Olmstead's latest handiwork. I knew you'd not do the right thing, get yourself a gun of some sort, so– Anyway, I also knew I couldn't stay away. Not after what I learned yesterday."

"You're right, Frank. I wouldn't have resorted to buying a gun. But tell us what you learned yesterday. Something new about Bryan? Where is he?"

Again Frank glanced briefly at Kathy. He knew of her sensitivity, and he chose his words carefully: "He apparently went up to Julian right after he escaped, and he killed Marge and Elaine Winters. You remember them, right? And then he went to Arizona and killed his own mother."

Arnold also looked in Kathy's direction. He had not told much of what he knew. "Let's take our coffee into the den, Frank," he said with a frown. "No need for Kathy to hear any of the details of–"

"You just stay right there!" Kathy said angrily, wagging the spatula in the direction of the two men. "I'd like to be treated as an adult, if you don't mind. Besides, breakfast is nearly ready, so get some plates out of the cupboard and the knives and forks too. You know where the ketchup is, Frank."

The two men exchanged knowing glances, but they did as they were told without question. As they ate, Frank continued telling what he knew. He withheld the gory details, but Arnold knew from the frequent hedging by his uncle that the murders of the two women in Julian, and of Bryan and Brendan's birth mother, had been particularly brutal.

"So they have no idea where he'll end up next; is that what Segura told you?" Arnold was now deeply concerned about the safety of Brendan's adoptive mother, and, in fact, Brendan himself, Becky and their two young boys.

"That's why I'm here," Frank said. "It's the only thing I could do. I was totally unsure when I'd get here. Hopped on a plane in Hartford, Connecticut, headed for Chicago, but there were no available seats on the flight from there to Portland. Long story, but I stood-by in Chicago and finally got a seat, last row in the damned plane. Hate that! I tried calling you from the plane, twice, but no luck. Then, it was nearly midnight local time when I got into Portland, so I stayed in a motel last night, right there at the airport."

"Hartford?" Kathy said. "Why Hartford?"

"We were on the road, heading for Cape Cod. Hilda drove the car on from there. She would have liked to come with me, but she'd promised her folks, so... Anyway, I'm happy she didn't come with me, really. In fact, you might want to consider joining her, Kathy." He eyed Arnold, who glanced at his wife, but knew that it would be a hard sell. "You ever been to the cape?"

Kathy said nothing.

"So how did you get to talk to Segura while you were on the road?" Arnold asked, mildly upset that Frank had not called to reveal his plans. "You break down and buy a cell phone?"

Frank laughed. "No. Hate the damned things! We stopped for lunch, called him from a pay phone. Getting harder all the time to find a pay phone these days. Have you noticed that? Never thought I'd see the day."

"Well, we're pleased you're here, Frank," Kathy said, passing around a small silver rack of toast.

"I suppose you brought your gun with you?" Arnold said. "How do you get on board a plane with a gun, these days?"

Kathy bristled visibly.

Frank's bushy black eyebrows lifted as he replied: "I pack it, disassembled, in checked baggage. That's about the only way, these days, even for a cop or any other licensed individual. You have to tell the airline, of course, and show your credentials."

Arnold knew that his uncle was a highly decorated former cop who eventually became a private eye after suffering a serious bullet wound in the hip. The limp he'd been left with was becoming more pronounced as Frank aged, but he never complained.

"I sure hope you don't have to use it," Kathy said. "I hate guns."

"I'll be nice, Kathy," Frank said with a grin. "Unless I get a serious chance to be nasty, that is. This Bryan Olmstead is an animal, sweetheart. He needs to be dealt with, or more people will die. You really should think of heading off someplace for a few days. If not Cape Cod, then maybe Florida? Your sister has family there, doesn't she? Seen them lately?"

Kathy's eyes flashed, but she didn't reply. There was an uncomfortable silence that seemed to last forever, and finally Arnold said, "So what's the plan? We just wait here, see if Bryan shows up, or what?"

"No, I think we should be proactive. We should try to use Brendan's psychic connection with his brother, maybe get some idea where he is. It'd be nice to head him off and nail him before he ever gets near this place."

"Think it'll work? Middlecoff's not here this time. I spoke with him yesterday, by the way, told him what was going on. He offered to come, but Brendan declined. Says he knows what's happening to him this time, with the dreams and everything."

"So he is dreaming again? Seen Bryan killing, has he? Anything like last time?"

"I don't know the details, Frank, but yes, yes and yes. We should maybe get together with him right away, huh?" Arnold looked at his watch.

"Where does he live?" Frank asked.

"A little more than an hour south of here. But his office is in Portland."

"I should call him," Frank said. "See what we can set up. I should also call Art Segura again, tell him I made it here safely. Hey, great breakfast, Kathy. Just what I needed to get the day started out right." He rubbed his stomach in appreciation, only his eyes showing the concerns he held.

## Chapter Eight

The media coverage of the brutal slaying of the Winters sisters was comprehensive. All the California newspapers saw it as front-page material, no doubt because of the nature of the murder of two middle-aged sisters, but papers all across the nation gave it some space; the radio and television news gave the story airtime, too. Most observers thought the motive for Bryan to kill the two women was flimsy. They had really played only a minor part in Bryan's original arrest. The San Diego area papers used the opportunity to sharply criticize the Sheriff's department for allowing Bryan Olmstead to escape while in their custody. This was the second high profile criminal to escape in similar circumstances in San Diego, and it gave the media the opportunity to level justified criticism at the embattled law-enforcement agency. In some of the stories, more ink was given to this aspect of the case than to the dreadful murders themselves, or the horror of what had happened to three new innocent and helpless victims. Actually, very few of the media accounts made mention of the murder of Sarah Olmstead, Bryan Olmstead's mother. A couple of newspaper articles did make this connection, despite the insistence of the Sheriff's spokesperson that there was still "no direct evidence" linking Bryan Olmstead to the Arizona murder. Cops in the various law enforcement agencies didn't buy this, however, and certainly not Art Segura.

Bryan Olmstead sat reading one such article about his activities; he was in the San Diego County Library, in Escondido. It was just three days after his escape, and he was quite pleased with all that he'd accomplished so far. He stroked his beard, acquired at a novelty store in Barstow earlier, and as he read the paper he smiled at the carefully veiled inference about the way he'd been treated as a child:

> Officials say Mrs. Olmstead raised her son in difficult circumstances and without help from the boy's father, who deserted them soon after the birth of the twin boys, Bryan and Brendan. 'She was not a perfect mother, by all accounts, but she did not deserve to die in this way,' Mohave County Sheriff Matt Henderson said. Henderson also cautioned that there was no direct evidence that Bryan Olmstead was the killer of his mother. The investigation continues.

Bryan put the newspaper aside and moved to a computer carrel, where he had serious work to do. He had an excellent memory for most things, but he'd forgotten the exact address where Brendan lived, his darling brother. While he was in the State Hospital he'd read a newspaper account of the way the goody-goody Brendan had used "psychic powers" to track down his own "evil twin." Whoever had written that article had broken the cardinal rule of not disclosing personal information about innocent people involved in crime stories in any way. They had actually stated the name of the street, *Fairhope,* an easy name to remember, but not the house number. Bryan felt sure that with a little effort and some imagination he would be able to locate his brother and deal with him next, or very soon.

He used Mapquest at first, and soon found out that Fairhope was a short street, which would make his task easier. He then went to the phone book white pages on-line. But this proved fruitless; there was no listing for a Carlson on Fairhope. But there was a B. Carlson on Sintonte Drive, in the same community of Rancho Bernardo. Quickly switching back to Mapquest, Bryan smiled in satisfaction as he discovered that Sintonte was a few short blocks away from Fairhope Road, and he wondered if maybe his brother had moved. *Or maybe the newspaper account had been in error?*

Bryan sat and thought for several minutes. How could he get the confirmation he needed? Was the B. Carlson on Sintonte Drive his brother? He wrote down the telephone number and looked around the library. No sign of a pay phone, but he knew there had to be one somewhere nearby. He didn't want to ask at the reference desk, his fake beard not being all that authentic, close-up.

He finally found a phone and made the call.

"Carlson's," a cheery female voice answered.

"Is this Mrs. Carlson?" Bryan asked, trying hard to sound friendly.

"Yes, it is. Who's calling?"

"My name is Adamson. Jerry Adamson, I believe I might have gone to school with your husband. At least, I hope I have the right Carlson. Is he there?"

"You must be looking for my son-in-law, Blake. No, he's not here right now, But Mary is. She's in the garden. I can get her if you hold on."

"Did you say your son's name is Blake, Ma'am? That's not the name of the Carlson I'm looking for. Do you have relatives in the area, by chance?"

"No, we don't. But there's another Carlson. We sometimes get the mail for a B. Carlson who lives not far from here."

"That could be the one," Bryan said, now excited. "You don't happen to have his phone number, do you? He's not listed in the phone book."

"Let me get my daughter," the woman said. "She might be able to help you. Just hold on for a second."

As Bryan waited, he glanced around the area he was now in, a kind of annex just off the entrance to the library. There were two pay phones, restrooms and a large rack of tourist information pamphlets. Coming out of the ladies restroom was a beautiful young woman, athletic and tanned. She was dressed in tight shorts and a sleeveless t-shirt that clung to her braless breasts in the most tantalizing manner. She tossed her long brown hair in a way that made Bryan start to think he should put his present plans on hold, follow this female and take her, the way he used to before–

"Hello, this is Mary." It was a vibrant young woman's voice in his ear.

"Hello, Mary," Bryan said, forcing himself to look away from the teasing rear end of the brunette as she walked away. "I'm sorry if I interrupted your gardening. Your mother said you might be able to help me. I'm trying to locate an old friend who–"

"Yes, Mother told me," Mary said. "I don't have the phone number for Brendan Carlson, but we do have their address, if that would help?"

***Help?*** Bryan couldn't believe his good fortune. It was Brendan! He quickly wrote down the address he was given, and in seconds he was back in his car. Well, not his car but one he'd "borrowed," the latest of several automobiles he had acquired to move around in. This particular one had been the easiest and best yet. He'd driven the side streets in the town of Barstow on his way back across the desert, looking for signs of folks away from home. He'd made a living in this way for some time, seeing the obvious signs: several newspapers lying on front lawns, on driveways or doorsteps. It was so damned easy. People were fools. At virtually every empty house he'd found something of value, but often cash in cookie jars, piggy-banks etc. Once he'd even been lucky enough to find some bearer bonds worth more than four thousand dollars. Always something!

The place in Barstow had been especially valuable because there was a car in the garage. Not just any car, but a pretty fancy car: a nearly new Buick with plenty of gas in the tank. The keys he'd found in the house! Such a deal! The owners either had another car, or they'd had someone drive them to the airport, or someplace. There was no cash in the house, but he did get a good feed in the kitchen and he also found a nicely detailed calendar on the wall. His benefactors not only left him transportation, they also informed him of their intention to stay away for another several days, on a cruise out of San Diego. So Bryan knew no one would be alerted to the car theft, not until he had moved forward with his plans to exact revenge and was long gone, far away, driving another new vehicle. There was also a useful bonus in this car: a cell phone!

He started the Buick and drove away from the library, scanning the map he'd printed out. Just a few blocks and he'd be there. Brendan and his family would not likely be home yet, but Bryan would wait. He'd greet them one-by one and enjoy himself destroying them in the most painful ways. He found himself wondering what Brendan's wife was like. She'd not be young—as he really liked them—but he would take her anyway. He was long overdue. The only question was would he do it after killing her, or before? With Brendan watching, while bleeding to death on the floor? Niceties like this he'd decide later. He wiped away the considerable drool that had accumulated on his chin and consulted the map, noting with envy the quality of neighborhood he was entering. "Sooo, my brother is doing alright for himself," he muttered as he parked a few yards past the address the helpful Mary had given him on the phone. "But you'll not be enjoying your wealth for much longer, Brendan."

Entry was easy for Bryan, and he soon found food and drinks, turned on the TV and waited for his prey.

## Chapter Nine

It was after ten o'clock in the evening when the phone call came to the Towncraft residence. "Want me to take it?" Frank asked, noting the look of anxiety on both Kathy and Arnold's faces. Arnold nodded his reply.

"Towncraft residence," Frank said sternly into the phone. He gave Arnold a thumbs-up sign and said, "Yes, Art. What's up?"

The Towncrafts spent the next five minutes trying to guess from Frank's cryptic comments and questions just what the news from Detective Segura might be. Frank's face revealed little, and he paced as he listened, but they were able to conclude there had been other murders, and they sat ashen-faced, waiting to hear the details. Finally, Frank hung up the phone, sat down and confronted them.

"Well," he said, infuriatingly deliberate, "if there was any doubt about what Bryan Olmstead's plans are, we can now be certain. He killed again today. The family that bought Brendan and Becky's house, down in San Diego. Four of them. A man, his wife and their two children, a teenage girl and a younger boy."

"Oh, my dear God!" Kathy's face was contorted with fear and horror.

Arnold wordlessly tried to comfort her, moving closer to her on the couch and embracing her, holding her head next his shoulder. She began to sob uncontrollably.

"I'm sorry to have created anguish for you," Frank said. "But there's no easy way to tell you what happened. This man has gone completely berserk. He's a maniac."

"Let me get you a glass of port wine, dear," Arnold said. "It'll settle you a bit maybe. I could use one too. How about you, Frank?"

"I'll get them," Frank said. "You just... just stay right there."

When he returned to the living room, Frank found that Kathy was no longer crying, but she looked dreadful. The shock of what she'd heard had been terrible for her, and she undoubtedly feared for her own life, and for Arnold's. She also knew that her fears for Brendan, Becky and their two lovely boys were well founded. She took the small glass of port from Frank and thanked him. "I'm sorry to be such a fool," she said quietly, "I don't know those poor people, but it was a dreadful shock. What about Brendan's friends? Their old next-door neighbors, Tim and Trish Bartholome, are they all right?"

"They've gone somewhere safe," Frank said. "Segura persuaded them to leave right away, and fortunately they managed to get away before this awful thing happened to their new neighbors."

"Too bad they didn't think to warn this innocent family. Just because they lived in Brendan's house! Is that the assumed motive, Frank, or what?"

"No, that's not it at all." Frank obviously found it difficult telling all he knew. The implications were just too appalling to contemplate. But he came out with it anyway: "Segura said it looks as if Bryan didn't know Brendan had moved up here, to Oregon. No way he could, I suppose, he's been in prison and the state hospital. Anyway, they're pretty sure he came to the house and lay in wait for Brendan and his family to come home. When the new owners of the house came home instead, one-by-one, he attacked them. Probably obtained information from them on where Brendan lives now. Killed all four of them in their living room. The same way he did the two women in Julian and..."

Frank could see that the port wine Kathy had taken was not powerful enough medicine to prevent her from becoming horrified all over again. She sat shaking, obviously in shock, now, her hands clasped firmly in front of her face, tears streaming down her cheeks and whimpering like a sick puppy.

Arnold was having his own difficulty, but again he tried to calm his wife. He had downed his port in a single gulp, and he reached out now and picked up Kathy's glass, still half-full. "Here, dear," he said. "Come on, drink down the rest of this. It'll help. Come on, please take a sip."

"Do you have a sedative in the house?" Frank asked. "Valium, or anything?"

"No, we have nothing like that," Arnold said. "This wine will have to do."

"I might have some, er... some Xanax in my bag. I'll go get some?"

When Frank returned from his room, a prescription vial in his hand, Arnold asked, "Should we be mixing these with alcohol, Frank?"

Frank laughed. "Looks to me like the little bit of alcohol Kathy has consumed would be of little effect. But just have her take one of these now, and a few more to keep handy, in case she needs them." He opened the small container and counted out six Xanax tablets and placed them on the table.

Arnold eyed his uncle strangely, but he chose not to ask the obvious question. Instead, he said, "Yeah. I suppose one will do, for now. But let's not make it any worse. Let's not talk any more about this matter tonight. Maybe in the morning you can bring me up to date on the details, but not now. Kathy has taken this news very hard." He looked at his wife and brushed aside a wisp of hair that had fallen across her tear-stained face. "Do you think we should maybe go to a motel for the night, Frank? There's a decent place a few miles west of here, I could call and get us–"

The telephone interrupted again, alarming them all. Frank answered it quickly. It was Segura again, and although Frank said very little to the detective, Arnold and Kathy could tell there was more bad news. After he hung up, Frank sat with them again, a very somber expression on his face. He paused, seeking the right words.

"Well, there's more proof that cell phones are a damned menace," he said.

Arnold looked quizzically at his uncle, so Frank continued: "It seems the young girl who moved into Brendan's old house had become very friendly with Tim Bartholome's girl, Marlie. The neighbor kid's name is Janey, or I should say was. The crime scene unit at the house picked up a message on Janey's answering machine, from Marlie. She told where she and her folks were headed: Las Vegas. They believe that message came at around the time Bryan was doing his nasty work at the house, so he probably put two-and-two together. Marlie even revealed where they were planning to stay: Caesar's Palace." Frank sighed deeply. "God, could this get any worse?"

There was a long silence, and then Kathy said, with obvious difficulty, "So you think Bryan knows who Tim is, Frank? I mean, how would he know about Marlie?" She was shaking again, her face ashen with grief and fear.

"No way of telling, for sure, but the police have assumed that he does. The only question is, even if he does know, will he head to Vegas first or come up this way to deal with Brendan and his family. We need to get word to Brendan and Becky without delay." Frank consulted his watch.

"Maybe we should get away, Frank, like you suggested earlier." Arnold's thin face was ashen and drawn. "As I said before, there's a nice motel not far–"

"No, Arnold. Not necessary, not yet," Frank said, interrupting. "No way Bryan could get up here any time soon. Anyway, he may not even know you and I had anything to do with his original apprehension. But we should let Brendan know what happened. I promised Segura I would. They should not remain in their home after tonight. If Bryan drove all day today he could be in Oregon sometime tomorrow morning. But don't you worry; I have my gun, loaded and ready. He comes anywhere near here he's a dead duck."

Kathy did not seem appeased, so Arnold persuaded her to take another of the Xanax and go to bed. She willingly complied, and as she reached the foot of the stairs, she shouted, "Frank, will you be sure to check all the windows and doors before coming upstairs. Arnold will arm the security system, won't you, dear? Please?"

They seldom remembered to turn on the alarm system. The builder of their home had persuaded them to include such a device, but before this they had never felt even slightly at risk out here in rural Oregon, miles from any urban center. Now, Arnold suddenly felt grateful they had gone along with the contractor's recommendation. He went to the entry hall and punched in the necessary code numbers to arm the system.

"What in heaven's name is this world coming to," Kathy said, as Arnold followed her upstairs."

"You staying up for a while, Frank?" Arnold shouted from the landing.

"Yeah. Why?"

"I thought maybe you'd call Brendan. It's late, but—"

"Sure. I'll do it. Don't you worry, guys, everything will be all right. Get a good night's sleep, if you can."

But they didn't. Kathy was restless all night despite the tranquilizers she had taken, and Arnold slept fitfully too, waking often and listening in paranoid fashion to every slight sound in the night, every vehicle that passed nearby. At some point they heard Frank use the toilet, and then, before it was daylight, they heard the thud of the newspaper on their front doorstep, the delivery vehicle's wheels crunching on their lengthy gravel driveway. They slipped into a deep slumber after that, exhausted, and they slept until 8:45. Most unusual for Arnold, who was often up and around well before by six each day. As they stirred they could smell breakfast frying, and they knew they would find Frank in the kitchen, preparing his celebrated omelets, the only thing he really knew how to cook. They dressed hurriedly, each pretending they had no real reason to feel anxious and afraid, but each feeling a little better than when they went to bed. Daylight always seemed to bring some comfort, no matter what.

"G'morning," Frank said cheerfully as they entered the kitchen. "Your timing's just perfect. Sit right down and I'll transport you to heaven with my special recipe. Something new this time: a combination of potatoes, tomatoes and cheese in the omelets a-la-Frank. With onions and garlic, of course. You'll love it! Pour me a coffee, will you, Kath."

Kathy was sorting out vitamin tablets for herself and Arnold, their daily regimen. This reminded Arnold of the Xanax Frank had brought with him, and he asked why.

"Er... well, to be honest, I'm a nervous flyer. Always have been. My doctor recommended Xanax, and it works very well. I take it every time I fly."

Arnold grinned. It seemed inconceivable that his tough old uncle, the one-time cop and man of steel, needed help before getting aboard an airplane. He said nothing, however, and seated himself for breakfast. The aromas were tantalizing and his appetite surprised him, considering their circumstances.

***

At the same time the Towncrafts and their guest were enjoying breakfast, in The Dalles, Oregon, Bryan Olmstead was eating huevos rancheros at a grimy place called Pepe's Café. He had driven just a few hours the prior day, then spent the afternoon at the equally grimy Pine Tree Motel, relaxing by the algae-infested pool, knowing there was no need to rush. He had a long drive to his next target, but time was on his side. He felt sure no one would even know of his activities the night before last, or that he was driving a vehicle stolen from the home of the vacationing Charles and Muriel Albright, who would be on a cruise for several more days. He smiled as he thought how clever he was. It would be days before anyone discovered his "mistake" in San Bernardino. He smiled even more as he thought of what he'd done to the rather lovely Maria Arcata, the dark-eyed wife of the new owner of brother Brendan's old home. He had also enjoyed their sweet daughter, Janey. What was she, maybe sixteen years old? Such a nice figure for a girl so young! He had especially enjoyed seeing the horror in the eyes of her father as he did the girl. Such pleasure! Such excruciating pleasure. He wondered why he had waited so long before indulging his fantasies in this way. After all, he was now forty-two years old. He had waited years; had not fully realized just how pleasurable it might be to watch someone watching someone else die, especially somebody they cared about. To watch a female die, a woman of any age, was a real turn-on for Bryan, but there was

78

just something delightful and deeply satisfying about watching real anguish in a third person's eyes as you killed or tortured, raped or mutilated. The key was in doing something that produced humiliation and abuse; make them suffer and then die in pain. The look in the watcher's eyes was such a turn-on, especially when you had some good heavy metal going. Metallica, maybe, or Ratt? Yeah, Ratt! He was drooling again, and he wiped the saliva from his chin with his sleeve, looking around. All he could see in the café were guys in denims, rough-looking construction workers. There was an elderly couple in a nearby booth, but other than that... Anyway, none of them paid Bryan any attention, so he turned his eyes back to the map he had on the table beside him. He must plan carefully.

***

The desk clerk at Ceasar's Palace was adamant: "No, sir. There is no-one staying at the hotel by the name of Bartholome."

Segura wondered if Tim and Trish had decided to use false names, and he hoped they had. That would help them a great deal. On the other hand, he really needed to find them, warn them. He persisted with the clerk"

"If someone had shown up late last night, without a reservation, would you have been able to take them?" he asked.

"I don't have any way of being sure about that, Detective. I came on duty this morning at six. At that time all the rooms were filled. We have three convention groups here, so there's a good chance we would have had no vacancies. Sorry I can't be of more help."

"Can you check to see if any guests gave a home address in Rancho Bernardo? That's in San Diego, California." Segura was reaching now, and he knew it.

After several minutes the clerk finally came back on the line and said, "Sorry sir, there's nobody checked in with a home address in Rancho Bernardo."

Segura thanked the patient young man and hung up the phone. He then spent several minutes trying to decide what to do. He realized he'd made a significant blunder, not getting a cell phone number from Tim Bartholome . He could use his own office to check with all the various cell phone companies that serviced the Southern California area, but that would consume too much time. He had little time to spare, and lives were at risk in Nevada somewhere. Also in Oregon. He cursed and lit up a big cigar. This was his way of relaxing, and he opened up the window behind him, knowing his colleagues would complain bitterly if he didn't. *What the hell to do? Was it his job to protect people in far-flung places?* To Serve and Protect has limits, surely! He was about to pick up the phone again when it rang anyway, startling him. It was Tim Bartholome.

"Jesus H. Christ," Segura said. "Where the hell are you?"

Tim laughed. "You told me not to tell you that, Detective."

"Yeah, yeah, but I know you're in Vegas, all right? So where are you staying?"

"You sound agitated. Has something else happened?"

Segura sighed, hesitating, not knowing how or whether to tell what had happened to Tim's next-door neighbors. Finally, he said, "Yeah, something very nasty. I suggest you use discretion in telling your wife and daughter about this, but your neighbors, the Arcatas, they were all victims of Bryan Olmstead last night. He paid them a visit expecting to find Brendan and his family there instead of these people."

The silence at the other end of the line told what a dreadful shock this had been to Tim Bartholome. "Tim? You okay?" Segura asked.

"I... I'm just so... they were our friends. Janey? My God, what happened to Janey, their daughter?"

"You alone, sir? I mean, is your wife listening? Your daughter?"

"No. They've gone shopping. We couldn't get into Ceasar's last night. They were full, so we checked in down the strip a bit, at MGM Grand. Why?"

"Janey's dead, sir. I'm sorry. We never even suspected Bryan would do what he did. We got you away, and were watching Emily Carlson closely. It never dawned on me he might– Listen, Tim, you've got to get a hold of your daughter. She placed a call to Janey Arcata last night, left a message telling where you were planning to stay. We think Bryan could have heard that message, and if he did he could be on his way to Vegas right now. Ceasar's is where he thinks you're staying."

Again a lengthy silence.

"Do you understand what I'm saying?" Segura said, almost shouting now.

"I do, but Bryan doesn't know anything about us, does he? Why would he want to harm me and my–"

81

"We're talking about a raving maniac here, Tim. Are you prepared to assume that Bryan means you no harm? He never had a grudge against the Arcata family either, that's for damned sure. They had absolutely no connection to Brendan other than they happened to buy his house. Now they are all stone dead, along with three others, and so far in this killing rampage that seems to be revenge based. Listen, round up your family and get the hell away from there, you hear me. Call me again later today. You will do this, right?"

Tim Bartholome was angry, confused, frightened and repulsed by what he'd learned. He promised to do what Segura had urged him to do and hung up, but he knew that finding Trish and Marlie would be a major challenge. They had to know what had happened, but how would he tell Marlie about Janey? He felt like crying, so deep was his anguish, but he had to act, and swiftly.

The indoor shopping mall at Ceasar's Palace is huge, and they had said they'd be gone for hours. *So now what? Surely Bryan Olmstead had no idea what they looked like? Or did he? Did Janey have a picture of Marlie? Could the insane killer have broken into their own home last night and found photographs of all of them? Did the police think to check his home, see if it had been entered? Should he call Segura back and ask him these questions?* Tim regretted not doing just that, asking these and several other burning questions while he had the chance, the answers to which would help him decide what to do next. He was a bright man, but now he felt confused, unusually befuddled, and yet he realized his immediate choices were critical, lifesaving, perhaps.

He tried calling Segura back, but failed to make contact. He left a brief message on the detective's voice mail, including his own cell phone number; and then, as he was pocketing his phone he remembered that all the major shopping malls had paging services. Of course! Why didn't I think of that right away? No problem at all!

Tim knew it was no more than half a mile from the MGM Grand to the mall at Caesar's, but he took a taxi anyway. No time to get his car from the immense parking lot, and he'd check out later, when he knew Trish and Marlie were safe. The taxi driver was obviously displeased with such a short trip, but he accepted the hefty tip with a grunt of thanks anyway. Tim rushed inside the mall, using the main entrance, near the hotel, and he asked the first employee he saw how he could get someone paged.

"There are courtesy phones everywhere," the overly made-up young blonde said.
"Look, see that alcove over there. You'll find them in there. The numbers are all posted."

Tim ran to the place she had pointed out, and in a few short minutes he had made his request. He stepped back into the main entrance area, where he'd told the customer service representative he would wait for Becky and Marlie. The seconds ticked by slowly, with Tim pacing, growing more anxious with each second. Finally, he heard the announcement and immediately fretted about two things he hadn't thought of: The message was so garbled he wondered if anyone could actually hear what was said. And what if Becky was inside one of the stores? Was the page audible in all locations? Then he had a truly horrible thought: What if Bryan was in this mall? What if he heard the page?

Ten minutes passed, with Tim checking his watch every few seconds, still pacing, wondering if he should request a new page. The first one had been repeated after a few minutes, but he was quite convinced no one could have heard it. Just as he was getting ready to go to the alcove again, however, he spotted Becky and Marlie coming toward him. They didn't seem at all hurried. They were laughing, in fact, as they moseyed along. He knew they both loved shopping. They each had a shopping bag filled with purchases, so they had made some progress in the short time they had been at it.

"Hey, Dad," Marlie said as she neared, her smile now gone. "You said there was no rush. So what's up now?"

"Yeah," Becky agreed. "Why the long face and the urgent message?"

"We have to leave," Tim said. "Right now! I'll explain later."

They grabbed a cab again, and in the short ride, whispering, Tim explained what was going on. Marlie looked sheepish when her father came to the part about the message she'd left on Janie's answering machine.

"I'm sorry, Dad," she said simply, but her eyes said more. She understood exactly how her simple attempt to make contact with her friend had increased their own chances of being found by the maniacal Bryan Olmstead, but she was also mortified by what she had learned of Janie's fate. She said nothing more for a while, not really listening as her father explained what he planned to do, and then she started to shake uncontrollably, and then she wept her heart out.

The crowd in the lobby paid little attention to the sobbing teenager and her parents as they made their way to the elevators. Trish attempted to console Marlie, but she herself was now terrified. Tim seemed composed, but his outward appearance did not reveal the terror that clutched his heart as they made their way to their room. He knew they had to pack their bags in a hurry and get the hell away from this place. *But where would they go?*

## Chapter Ten

Suzie Carrow was never late for work, so Jeb Almont was worried about her. He had called her apartment already, but there was no answer. Jeb had a serious crush on his young receptionist, and although he'd never acted on his desires, he sure fantasized a great deal. Her young body, so lush and full, her sparkling blue eyes and vibrant personality... they teased him endlessly. Jeb's wife had seen the way he looked at Suzie, and she wondered sometimes what he would do if he ever got the chance. She was pretty sure her husband had been faithful to her, but she also knew men. Some men were not corruptible, perhaps, but Jeb? She had seen him pull a few stunts that were a little less than ethical in their twenty-two years in business together, so just what were his limits? They owned a small-town newspaper, and Jeb occasionally omitted a negative story about a friend or associate, or he published an overblown story when it involved someone they didn't care for. But Angie Almont knew, and took consolation in the fact that the local beauty queen they had hired, six months ago, would see nothing appealing in her balding middle-aged hubby. Jeb had not taken good care of himself, and he looked even older than any forty-seven year-old should. Suzie could do much better; Angie knew that. Even in this one-horse town, Warm Springs, Oregon.

"She'll be here, Jeb," Angie said. "Don't fuss. Did you see the quarter-page advertisement we got this morning? Ten straight weeks."

"What? Oh, no, I didn't." Jeb's distraction was obvious. "Who?" he added.

"The new restaurant that opened up out on the highway, near the turkey farm. *The Cooked Goose.* We should try it sometime. Folks say they have real good food and friendly service. Tracy Barker works out there as a hostess."

Jeb was not listening. He had gone to the window and was looking down onto the street from the second floor offices he and Angie rented for the *Gazette,* their weekly tabloid. He knew that Suzie usually parked her Honda Civic on the empty lot across the street. No sign of her little blue car, however.

"You suppose her mother might know where she is?" he asked vaguely.

Angie laughed. "I doubt it. You know that old biddy's been slowly drinking herself into oblivion. I doubt if she even knows where she is herself this time of the morning. Come on, Jeb, get busy. You have that article to finish. We have to be ready to take this layout to the printers tomorrow. "I'll answer the phones and such."

Jeb saw Deputy Tubbs' Crown Victoria flash by in the street below, going way too fast for his morning trip to Winchell's Donuts, at the north edge of town, and he had a nasty premonition. But he returned to his desk anyway and he sat down, tried hard to focus on his computer screen. He did indeed have an article to write, about the plans the county had for building a new library in town–something Jeb and Angie had been lobbying for since way before they bought out the original owners of the *Gazette*. He glanced at his wife, wondering if she could read his mind, but Angie was hard at work.

Jeb didn't get many more words written in the next fifteen minutes. He poured fresh coffe into his mug and sat back in his chair, thinking, and then he heard the wail of the siren on Hummell Mortuary's old Cadillac hearse. It served as an ambulance for this small community on rare occasions, Sam Hummell being a trained first responder as well as an undertaker. Even more rarely, his 1964 hearse served to deliver a human body to the county morgue, twenty miles away. Jeb just knew his premonition was valid: something awful had happened to his Suzie. Grabbing his jacket and the keys to his car, he said to Angie, "I'm going after that damned old meat wagon. I have a hunch there's a story out there."

It didn't take long for Jeb to catch up to the ancient Caddy, but soon after he did old Sam Hummell slowed down and turned his lumbering vehicle into a narrow dirt road. Jeb followed, hanging back a bit to avoid the cloud of dust that swirled up, and he realized this was the lane to Henry Serbein's farm. He knew Henry and Martha were away, visiting family in Omaha, so what the hell could be going on here? He tried to ignore the strong smell of onions. The Serbeins focused their efforts almost entirely on the production of onion seed, and on certain days in the late summer, when the wind was just right, you could smell the rotting husks all the way to the Jefferson County Seat, in Madras. That was nearly twenty miles away.

At the farmhouse, one of the oldest in the entire area but still in pretty good shape, Jeb parked well away from the other cars, next to the Serbein's big solitary barn, and he pulled out his notepad and a pen. He was now certain that a human body lay in that house, but who was it? That was the question. He knew the next few minutes would be extremely difficult to deal with, but he was, after all, a professional newspaperman. It was his responsibility to obtain the story and tell it to the 800-odd readers of the *Gazette*. Jeb had actually worked on a major newspaper for a while, years back, in Seattle, but he had missed the small-town life a great deal, and he missed even more his old girlfriend, Angie Saxon. He came home and married Angie, then the two of them had spent a few years raising the necessary cash to buy the town newspaper. Eighteen years had passed, and their big dreams for the paper had never quite been realized. But the two remained conscientious anyway.

Jeb reluctantly climbed out of his car and made his way toward the farmhouse. Right next to the house he could see the sheriff's vehicle, Hummell's black hearse and a brand new Chevy Malibu, silvery blue, no plates on it yet. Seated on the front stoop was a man he thought he might have seen before but couldn't place.

As he approached, Jeb could hear the muffled voices of Tommy Tubbs and Sam Hummell inside the house, and he wondered just exactly what they had found. *And just who the heck was this guy sitting on the porch?*

"Mornin'" the man said. "You with the Sheriff's department?"

"Me? No, I'm Jeb Almont, Editor of the *Gazette*. Well, I'm the editor, publisher, reporter and general dogs body. What's going on here? And who are you?"

The man stood up and reached out for a handshake. "Mort Stadler," he said. "State Farm Insurance. The Serbeins have been my customer for many years."

This insurance agent couldn't be more than thirty years old, Jeb thought, so he found it unlikely that the "many years" could be that large a number.

"Henry and Martha are away," Jeb said.

"Yes, sir, I found that out when the deputy showed up. I called him on my cell phone after I found the body in there?"

"You found a body in there? How'd you get inside?"

Stadler laughed nervously and said, "The door was wide open. Nobody answered when I called out, so I went over to the barn, checked there first and then I came back here, to the house, and went on inside. That's when I saw her. Oh, Lordy!"

"Her?"

"There's a dead girl in there. A young woman, naked. It's not a sight you'd want to see, Mr. Almont. There's blood all over the place. I've never seen anything like it."

Jeb toyed with the idea of going inside, but he knew the sheriff would be angry if he did. They had crossed swords a few times over such transgressions, the deputy accusing the newspaperman of sticking his nose into police business. Not that there had been homicides, there were none in this small community, but Jeb had run afoul of the sheriff over break-ins and less serious crimes. "The public has a right to know, Deputy," Jeb always said. But he decided he'd wait outside this time; and besides, he felt decidedly ill-at-ease. Anyway, there was likely more he could glean from this young insurance salesman.

"Why did you assume I was with the sheriff's department?" Jeb asked.

"I heard the deputy tell the medical examiner he'd called in somebody from the county headquarters. Told me they'd likely send a homicide detective to interrogate me after they'd examined, er, the body and such."

Jeb grinned and pointed at Sam Hummell's hearse. "That old bucket belongs to the local undertaker. Sam has some training in triage, but he's not the coroner. He gets called out at times like this, and he's glad to do it. He knows there's sometimes business to be had when the dust is all settled. The Chevy yours?"

"Yes, sir, I just picked it up last–"

At that moment Tommy Tubbs emerged, grimfaced and obviously shaken. He didn't seem a bit surprised to see Jeb on the porch. "Morning, Jeb," he said, interrupting the insurance man. "What led you to this sorry event? You know who's in there?"

"I saw you fly right on past the donut shop, Tommy. A rare event. Then old Sam's homemade siren woke up the town. Had to be something big going on. I know Martha and Henry are away, so who is it?"

Tubbs hesitated, not anxious to see this story in the newspaper. He also felt it was not beyond the realm of possibilities that Jeb Almont knew something about this crime. After all, the victim worked for the newspaper. No telling what might have been going on between Jeb Almont and young Suzie Carrow.

"You're going to have to wait on that, Jeb. Sorry. We need to get a crime scene unit here, and no doubt they'll want me to get the victim properly identified. Why don't you go on back to town? I'll have more information for you tomorrow, likely. You've done enough damage here already; probably fouled up the tire tracks in the road."

"Morning, Jeb," Sam Hummell said, coming from inside. "You got here in a hurry. Come to take in a whiff of the rotting onions, did you? Sorry to say your receptionist will not be into work today. Not tomorrow neither." The rotund undertaker evidently had no knowledge of the sheriff's intention to withhold the name of the victim.

"Suzie?" Jeb demanded. "You can't be serious, Sam. Suzie Carrow? He suddenly felt a wave of nausea, and fear. Or was it just shock? Either way, he knew he had to sit down. There was an old overstuffed settee on the porch, and he made his way to it, sat, and placed his head between his knees and took several deep breaths. This was not exactly the story he had been hoping for. *My God! Suzie was dead?*

\*\*\*

Brendan was quite pleased to be invited to spend time with Arnold and Kathy Towncraft. He was also comforted to learn that Frank Dobson was there too–the old ex-cop from Pittsburgh who had a tough demeanor but seemed to reek of security and integrity. Rebecca had protested, mildly, but she had willingly helped Brendan pack their bags and pull together some books and other school materials for the boys. As a former teacher, she was able to convince the school principal that she could home school Jason and Tommy while they were away. She had described the reason for their departure as a "family emergency," and it really was. When discussing the whole nightmarish turn of events in front of the two boys they had exercised great caution. No sense alarming them, so they simply said they were going to visit with friends for a few days.

The Towncrafts were also pleased to have Brendan's family as houseguests, especially Kathy. But even Arnold felt a certain sense of protective paternalism. Brendan was like the son he'd never had, and a fine substitute for the students he sometimes missed. He never admitted to others that he missed his work as a professor, but in quiet moments he acknowledged it to himself.

The Carlsons had finished unpacking their bags and settled into two rooms in the Towncrafts spacious home, and Kathy had taken the two boys and their mother down the garden to show off her greenhouse. Brendan joined Arnold and Frank in the professor's study. Frank had every intention of attempting to induce Brendan into a hypnotic trance, so that they could seek clues as to Bryan's current activities and whereabouts, but Brendan preempted such an attempt.

"He's done it again," he said bluntly, as soon as they were settled. He didn't seem particularly perturbed, which surprised Arnold.

"My God!" Towncraft said. "You had another dream?"

Brendan sat down and poured coffee from the decanter Frank had brought in.

"Not a dream, Arnold," he said. "A waking vision. I had them before, remember? This time I was sitting on the toilet, just sitting there, not even trying to make contact with Bryan. And it happened." He grinned. "The vision, I mean."

"Tell us what you saw," Frank said, ignoring the tasteless and out-of-place double entendre, pulling out a pencil to make notes.

"Well, to be honest, it's not exactly like 'seeing' something. It's more like experiencing it, as if it was something happening to me. The first time it happened I thought I was going nuts, but now... Well, I know what's going on."

"So tell us the details," Towncraft said impatiently.

"Sure. Well, I was inside this house, a farmhouse. All the furniture seemed old fashioned. You know, dark woods, heavy dresser and so on. She was tied to a chair, at first, and–"

"She?" Towncraft's impatience was matched in Frank. "Describe the woman, Brendan."

"Pretty. Attractive, young, blonde hair, blue eyes. I can still see her eyes. Terrified eyes."

"She was tied up? What about her clothes?" Frank was scribbling furiously, his keen focus in evidence.

"Totally naked. She had no clothes."

In Brendan's first series of contacts with his evil twin, in scary episodic trances, dreams and visions, Professor Ruben Middlecoff had successfully coached him into pushing aside his sense of terror and the horrific sights he seemed to be a part of, focusing instead on the details of the scene's periphery. It was now evident that Brendan had retained that ability, was doing it extraordinarily well.

"Were there any sounds, Brendan?" Frank asked.

"No, not that I can recall."

"What did he do? I mean, what happened next?"

"Well, like all the other times, he raped her. He undid the ropes that held her in the chair, threw her down and raped her. Her hands were still tied by her sides, like this," he demonstrated. "The rope was wrapped several times around her waist."

Brendan was remarkably cool, and Frank felt this was good. All the more likely he would remember important details. "Did she scream or make any other sounds?" he asked.

"No. She had a gag, a wad of some sort in her mouth, held in place with string, looked like twine."

"Twine?"

"Yes, that stringy, coarse, yellowish stuff farmers use?"

"How do you know that?" Frank asked. "You raised on a farm or something?"

Brendan smiled. "I had a friend whose uncle had a farm, in Colorado. I used to go there for a week or two every summer. He raised cattle. Had some cash crops, too, and I helped, sort of. Mostly just had fun."

"Colorado?"

"Yeah. Not far from Grand Junction."

"Any sense of where you were in your vision?"

"No, other than–"

The telephone rang and all three men exchanged apprehensive glances. Frank nodded slightly and Arnold picked up the phone. "Towncraft," he said.

"It's for you, Frank. Detective Segura." He turned the phone over to his uncle.

Frank said very little for the next couple of minutes, obviously listening intently, occasionally grunting an acknowledgement. Finally, he thanked Segura for the update and hung up.

"What's going on?" Brendan asked. During the phone call his growing concern had been evident, his face a picture of uncertainty and apprehension as he attempted to comprehend.

"Nothing new on Bryan," Frank said, "and I suppose that's the good news. But when he was doing what he did in your old home, Tim and his family had their whereabouts accidentally revealed, or potentially so, by their daughter, Marlie. She left a phone message at the Arcata's, for young Janie" His eyes dwelt on the younger man for a few seconds, and he seemed uncertain how to proceed. But he finally did: "So they now suspect he knows where you live, and also where the Bartholomes went to get away from danger. He could have obtained all the information he needed to find you from the people who... er... from the Arcatas."

"So he may be on his way here, or he could choose to go to Las Vegas," Brendan said glumly. "But surely they've moved on by now, so—"

"How did you know they went to Vegas?" Frank asked.

"I called Tim on his cell phone, right after you told me what had happened in our old house. He brought me up to date on his plans, told me where he was headed next."

Frank looked puzzled. "Tim said nothing about the phone message to your old house?"

"No. Probably doesn't know about it."

"But Segura said he'd told Tim all about it, used that information to scare him into moving on."

"Tim maybe wanted to spare you, Bren," Arnold said.

Frank grunted, seeming deep in thought. "Did you talk to the young girl, Brendan? What's her name? Marlie, is it?"

"Yeah, short for Marlene. No, I didn't talk to her. Tim did say she's really upset. Almost hysterical. They're all scared. I just assumed... She and the Arcata girl were good friends, I suppose, so that explains it. She may also feel bad about the message."

"Call him again, Brendan. Tell him to find a place to park his car, somewhere public, and then he ought to take a taxi to someplace he can rent another car. He shouldn't be driving his own vehicle." Frank's concern was obvious.

"You think Bryan knows what kind of vehicle Tim and his family are driving," Brendan asked. "How would he know that?"

Frank hesitated, looking at Arnold and then at Brendan. "Would you want to chance it? For the sake of a few days rental on a car? No telling what information he got out of the Arcata family before he killed them."

"But there's no way Bryan would even know anything about Tim and Trish. How could he? Unless the phone message..."

Frank hesitated again before responding: "Yeah. Like I said, would you want to chance that?"

Brendan stayed quiet for a few seconds, and then he went looking for his cell phone. While he was out of the room Arnold said to his uncle, "You're being overly cautious, Frank. There is really no way Bryan could know about Tim and Trish. The phone message would mean very little to him, even if he heard it. I'm surprised Segura urged the Bartholomes to leave town at all."

"There's something I didn't tell you, Arnold. Didn't want to give Brendan any more reasons to worry. Segura told me there was a young woman killed and raped in Las Vegas last night. No proof yet, but it matches the MO of the most recent nasty work done by Bryan Olmstead."

Arnold was obviously shocked, but he also felt some slight sense of relief. If this latest killing really was the work of Bryan, it meant that he'd gone after the Bartholomes and will not soon be in Oregon. Maybe, with a little luck, the police might catch him before he turned his attention to his targets to the north. He realized he was being selfish.

"Surely a woman getting killed in Las Vegas is not all that unusual," he said.

"This one was particularly brutal. Same kind of knife mutilation; the abdominal area. Evidence of anal rape. Bryan's particular brand of bestiality and misogyny seems to be written all over it."

"You think he's a psychotic woman-hater Frank?"

"Doesn't seem to be much doubt about that. The police profilers have apparently come to that conclusion. An abusive mother who was as immoral as they come, and brutal to the boy. His pent up hatred, without action or psychological help for many years... there's no evidence Bryan ever formed a meaningful and healthy relationship with any woman. Classic case."

At that point Kathy and Becky came in with the two boys and Kathy called out, "Who'd like some hot apple cider?"

Frank looked at Arnold and grinned. "We should be as lighthearted as Kathy is trying to be," he said. "Let's join in the charade. We can continue working with Brendan a little later."

"I suppose you're right," Arnold said. "Anyway, it seems like the heat is off, for now; at least up here. Seems likely that Bryan is still in Nevada."

Frank didn't reply, and the two of them went to the kitchen. There, Brendan's two young boys seemed as genuinely lighthearted as their mother and "Aunt" Kathy were pretending to be.

"I have some freshly baked oatmeal cookies to go with the cider," Kathy said, and the boys whooped their enthusiastic endorsement.

Kathy had no children of her own, so she would never experience the joys of grandchildren. But she had become so fond of Brendan and Rebecca that they seemed like her family, and these two lively and likable young boys, Tommy and Jason, she embraced with grandmotherly affection. Just knowing they were safe, not off in their own home where they would be vulnerable, made Kathy almost forget that a devious and clever killer could probably track them down anyway, even here.

For the next two hours, the seven denizens of the Towncrafts home enjoyed a variety of pursuits designed to sustain a light-hearted atmosphere. Brendan had made contact with his pal, Tim, again and was satisfied that the Bartholomes were safe, on their way to an unspecified location in a rented car. Marlie's cell phone had been confiscated by her father, so she could do no more damage with it. Tim had assured Brendan he would be in touch again in a day or two.

Brendan did have one other unselfish concern: his adoptive mother, Emily Carlson, now in her seventies. She remained stubbornly resistant to travel, or to go into hiding anywhere, and each time Brendan spoke with her she sounded dismissive of the notion that she could be in danger. The police had assured Brendan her house was under surveillance, so that helped somewhat, but all kinds of doubts lingered in Brendan's head. Should he just go get her, bring her here? That would be an extra burden on the Towncrafts. All their bedrooms were now taken, anyway. He decided he would trust in the promises of Detective Segura.

After a game of "States & Capitals," at which Jason excelled, beating everybody else, the three men declared they had work to do, and again they went to Arnold's study. They closed the door, intent on developing a proactive strategy. First, however, Brendan revealed that he'd had yet another waking vision.

"This was almost identical to the first," he said. "This time, however, the brutality was much worse. After the rape, I... he started beating her with his fists. He actually knocked her unconscious. She was bleeding from the mouth and nose, and... it was incredibly graphic. I can't begin to tell you how this made me feel. He's just inhuman, a beast of the worst kind." Brendan was visibly shaking by the time he'd finished this brief account, and there were tears in his eyes.

Arnold came to his side, where he was seated, and he silently squeezed the younger man's shoulder. "I feel for you, Brendan," he said. "I wish there was some way we could prevent you from going through these experiences."

Frank was no less sympathetic, but he was more pragmatic than his nephew.

"Let's not wish for an end to these visions just yet," he said. "Remember how useful they were last time? I'm still hopeful we can learn something informative, something that will help us find this bastard before he finds us. Brendan, think carefully. Where were you when this happened; this latest vision?"

"I was outside, getting something I left in the car. I opened up the trunk and bent over to grab my briefcase. Suddenly I was back in that same place. The one I told you about earlier. The farm house." Brendan shook his head, seemingly trying to reject the awful sights he'd seen, the experiences he'd been a part of. He closed his eyes for a few seconds, sitting perfectly still.

Arnold looked at Frank, expecting him to ask more questions. But Frank held up a hand to silence Arnold. He wanted to allow Brendan these few moments of comfortable retreat; or maybe he was hoping Brendan would recall some small detail that might be valuable. Finally, Brendan opened his eyes and he silently looked at his host. "He killed her," he said, almost dispassionately. He was obviously becoming somewhat desensitized to even the worst elements of these experiences. Or maybe he was developing sufficient discipline to control his emotions.

"He raped her again," he said. "And then he... he took a knife and stabbed her in the abdomen, many times. She died quite quickly, but the horror in her eyes revealed the shock and the pain she suffered."

Frank suddenly appeared intense, focused in a way that Arnold had seen many times before. "Can you tell us anything about the room she was in? How about the carpet, or whatever the floor is? How about the furniture? What kind of–"

"Oriental rug," Brendan said. "She was lying on an ornate rug, mostly a dark green, with red and beige geometric patterns and swirls. It became heavily stained with her blood, and there was some trickling off the edge, onto the hardwood floor."

"Anything else, Brendan? Anything at all?"

"Onions."

"Onions?" Frank glanced at Arnold, who seemed equally puzzled. "You could see onions? Where? What kind?"

"I could smell them. A very strong smell." He shook his head again, obviously confused. "How is it possible? How I could smell onions?"

Kathy had started preparing dinner in the kitchen, and there were tempting aromas penetrating this room, now, and Arnold wondered if these current smells were confusing Brendan.

"If you remember, Brendan," Arnold said, "you smelled things last time. Middlecoff explained it in his usual manner, with scientific names for the–"

"An olfactory response triggered by extrasensory stimuli," Frank said, matter of fact.

Arnold knew that his uncle had an extraordinary memory, but he often also demonstrated a remarkable depth of understanding in many fields. He smiled at Frank, but he said nothing. Didn't want to break the man's concentration.

"Onions cooking, Brendan?" Frank asked. "Like you can smell now, from the kitchen?"

Brendan shook his head, "No, I don't think so. Not like that. Anyway, I was outside, remember? So, no. It was raw onions. Lots of them. Heavy smell. Stale raw onions. Rotting, maybe"

"And you think this house they were in is a farm house?"

"Yes. It just had that feel to it. Old, small rooms, dark and well-worn wooden plank flooring. And the windows were small, wooden casements."

"You saw windows? Could you see outside?"

Brendan didn't respond immediately. He closed his eyes again, as if concentrating. Professor Middlecoff had coached him into doing this the last time around. There was a breathless silence for a few seconds, and then Brendan opened his eyes wide.

"There was a barn," he said. "A big one, in good shape. Steel sides and roof."

"So it was a farm," Arnold said.

"Maybe a farm that grows onions," Frank added.

Their session was interrupted by the telephone. Arnold picked up before the second ring and said gruffly, "Towncraft." He quickly turned the phone over to Frank, saying, "Segura again."

The information that Frank gleaned from the detective this time was mostly insignificant; in fact it seemed evident that the purpose of his call was to see if Frank had anything new to report. Arnold wondered, as he listened, if Frank would say anything about the latest visions Brendan had experienced, and about the onion farm possibility. He soon got his answer.

"Yes, Art, we've been busy with Brendan. He and his family joined us here, at Arnold's place. And it seems certain he has experienced some new psychic connections with his brother. Bryan has killed again."

Frank listened for a second or two, and then he said, "Yes, there seems to be no doubt about it. A young woman, a pretty blonde, killed in a farmhouse somewhere. And Brendan smelled onions, lots of raw onions, so I think it might be an onion farm. Other than that, we– What?"

Again, it seemed Segura had questions, and no wonder. No doubt he was startled by what he'd heard and needed more information–lots more. Frank listened in silence for a while, and then he said, "Not so far. All I can tell you is that it was a blonde girl in a farmhouse somewhere. Oh, and there's a big steel barn That, and the onion smell; that's all I can–"

"A Buick, Frank.," Brendan said, agitated. "Tell him Bryan is driving a Buick." Brendan had grabbed Frank by the arm, anxious to add this bit of information.

Frank looked puzzled, but he passed this revelation to Segura anyway, and the detective asked several more questions that Frank could not answer. "You know what kind of Buick, Brendan?" Frank asked. "Color, maybe?"

Brendan shook his head. "That's all I have," he said.

Frank hung up he asked Brendan how he knew about the Buick.

"I just remember seeing the triple shield logo thing, in the center of the steering wheel, as I... as he drove away. This is all so vague, really, but I remember that little detail. I used to drive a Buick at one time. They all have that same emblem."

Frank grunted in apparent confusion. He paused for a second or two, thinking deeply, and then he reported that there were now three sets of state law enforcement agencies with APB's out on Bryan Olmstead: California, Arizona and Nevada. There was also the San Diego County Sheriff's department, of course, and it seemed to Frank as if Segura was the only one focusing his entire efforts on the case.

"Why Arizona, Frank?" Arnold asked.

"It's automatic. Even though they all now know that Bryan had only one probable victim in Arizona – his mother. She was his likely target and certainly is dead; that's the reason they're involved."

"Have they actually established that Bryan killed her, Frank?" Brendan asked.

Frank wondered just how much of an emotional impact Brendan felt over the slaying of his natural mother. *Probably none,* he surmised, but he certainly seemed to be terribly upset that his twin was on a killing spree again, had killed at least six people since escaping and had continued killing for mere sport, regardless of the victims' identity or their involvement in his original arrest.

"They found a couple of partial fingerprints that almost completely prove that Bryan was in the house, in Kingman," Frank said. "And since his mother moved into that home while Bryan was incarcerated, I'd say that pretty much establishes his guilt."

It was apparently dinnertime, signaled by a cheery "Come and get it," from the kitchen. Arnold knew that Kathy was a long way from the persona she was bravely projecting, but he was proud of her for the way she was dealing with everything.

Similarly, conversation at the dinner table was lighthearted and, at times, quite humorous. Tommy soon proved to those who did not know him well that he was as bright as his big brother, and very funny. Both boys were well behaved, and had impeccable table manners for youngsters. Although you could see by the look on their faces that Brussels sprouts were not their favorite food, they dutifully ate the three small ones Kathy had placed on their plates. "I like the meat, Mrs. Towncraft,"

Jason said, making it clear that everything else on his plate could have been withheld.

"Thank you, Jason," Kathy said. "Do you like Pasta? I thought we might have that tomorrow night."

"Pasta's fine. I also like Macaroni and cheese."

Kathy grinned at the boy. "It's really the same thing," she said. "Just different shapes. Maybe we'll have that one day soon, but tomorrow I'm going to make some marinara sauce. Arnold loves that."

"How long are we going to live here?" Tommy said, and that seemed to remind the adults of the reason they were all together, but what could they say to these boys? Brendan looked at Arnold, and he seemed ready to provide an answer, but Arnold beat him to it: "You just got here, Tommy," he said. "We hope you'll stay with us for several more days."

Brendan winked at his benefactor and smiled at Tommy. "Did you know that Dr. Towncraft was a professor," he said, trying desperately to change the focus of his son's thinking. "He has written many books and is quite a famous man."

"I thought you were a doctor," Tommy said. "I saw it on some of your mail. Is that why you came to us when Mommy was asleep all that time?"

Arnold grinned. "No, Tommy, I'm not that kind of a doctor. I was a teacher in a college. A professor, not a medical doctor. There are many different kinds of doctors."

"But you did help bring Mommy back from where she went."

Arnold seemed embarrassed. "Not really," he said. "My friend, Professor Middlecoff, he helped the most. He's another kind of doctor. A psychologist."

Tommy went quiet for a while, and Towncraft assumed the boy had put the matter out of his head, perhaps confused by what he'd heard. But he was wrong. Tommy said something that surprised everyone, especially his mother:

"I want to be a piecogolist when I grow up. If they help people who get hurt, like Mommy, that's what I want to do."

There was a second or two of silence, everyone taking in what the youngster had said. Then, Kathy, who had the glisten of tears in her eyes, said, "How sweet that is, Tommy. I bet you'd be a good 'piecogolist.' And that would make your mom and dad very proud, no doubt." She smiled at Rebecca.

Rebecca smiled back, and she too had a tear forming. "It sure would, Tommy," she said. "But both you boys can be whatever you want. I'll always be proud of you, no matter what you choose to do. You know that, right?"

Dessert was a classic apple crumble, with vanilla ice cream, and everyone praised Kathy lavishly for her cooking skills. The two boys made it clear that even the requirement of downing Brussels sprouts was a small price to pay for this final treat. They both asked for second helpings.

After dinner, Frank cajoled Arnold and Brendan into doing the cleanup work. They faked a protest, but then they relented and ushered the two women off to play more games with Tommy and Jason. In the kitchen, as they worked, the three men resumed their discussion of the reason they were all together.

There were really two reasons, each manifest in the other: They sought mutual comfort and protection that comes in numbers, but they also knew they were obligated to try to find constructive ways to help in the apprehension of a depraved killer. No easy assignment. They finished loading the dishwasher and cleaning up the pots and pans, talking all the time in hushed tones. But they really reached no meaningful conclusion about how to proceed.

**Chapter Eleven**

They spent most of that evening on the Internet, Brendan working with his laptop computer, dial-up connected through Arnold's phone line, while Arnold sat with Frank at his desktop unit on a direct service line. Brendan's unit had a wireless card built in, but he couldn't seem to configure it properly for access through Arnold's router. He said he'd call a friend for some advice the next morning, so that he could take advantage of the faster speed of DSL.

But it was Brendan, despite working with a slow dial-up connection, who was the first to come up with something potentially useful. He had been checking with various agencies of government in Nevada, Oregon and California, seeking information on where onions are a major cash crop. At first this trail had been so winding and seemingly endless that he was almost ready to give up. And then, quite suddenly, he said, "Hey, take a look at this, guys. I found out there's something special about farming for the production of onion seed, as opposed to onions themselves." He brought his notebook computer to Arnold's desk, trailing the phone line, and the three of them pored over what Brendan had found. It was an elaborate website devoted to the production of onion seed, the host being the University of California, Davis.

"Where is Davis, Brendan?" Frank asked, preparing to make notes again.

"Near Sacramento. UC Davis is recognized as one of the top agricultural universities in the country, and for many other disciplines, of course. Good medical school too."

"And what's so interesting?" Arnold asked.

"I found a brief article about the method used for drying onion seeds, and it triggered a memory from my vision. I saw a large agricultural trailer next to the barn, and on the trailer was a pile of folded yellow blankets; well, they looked like blankets to me. But I now suspect they were tarpaulins."

"Nothing unusual about tarpaulins on a farm, is there?" Frank said.

"But there were hundreds of them, Frank. Stacked up on top of the wagon."

"Hundreds?"

"Had to be. And look what it says here: They dry the onion seeds by spreading them a few inches thick, on tarpaulins, on the ground. The seeds dry in the sun, and they rake them over several times to get them all exposed sufficiently."

"But surely onion seeds don't have an aroma, do they? You said you smelled the onions."

"Right, Frank, and no doubt the seeds have all been dried by now, anyway. That's why the tarps were all folded, ready to be stored away. Look, it says that the season for production is late

July, and it's now the middle of August. The sun is at its hottest in July, best for drying, so–"

"But what of the smell, Brendan," Arnold asked. "Frank must be right, onion seeds don't have much of an aroma."

Brendan patiently scrolled down the website, looking for a vital link.

"Look," he said, pointing. "Read what that says, right there."

Towncraft adjusted his glasses and started to read to himself, but Frank nudged him. "Read it aloud, Arnold," he said. "So we can all hear."

Arnold knew his uncle needed reading glasses–and no wonder, being in his mid-seventies. But Frank was too stubborn to wear them all the time. Anyway, the font on the web page was really quite small. Arnold had a little trouble reading it himself:

"Okay, Old Timer," he said. "I'll paraphrase though, because there's a lot of technical jargon in here. It says the Allium Cepa seeds, that's the Latin name for onions, I suppose. Anyway, the seeds grow in something called 'umbrells.' That must be the name of the round cluster-of-a-thing that onions produce when you leave them in the ground and they go to seed. The timing for harvesting seeds is critical, it says here, and if left too late the mature seed will scatter in the wind, and if–"

"Not that part, Arnold," Brendan said. "Look, down here, beginning right there." He pointed.

"Okay, I see it. The spent onions themselves have no commercial value and most onion seed farmers simply plough them into the ground and allow them to putrefy, as fertilizer for the next crop. Though they then often find it necessary to plough lime into the soil, to balance the Ph, this practice is found to be less expensive than removing the spent onions and disposing of them in some eco-friendly way. Yat-ta-da-da, wait a minute… lots of jargon here. Okay, it then goes on to give all kinds of statistical information on yield per acre, weather related variables and there's even a list of pests farmers need to eradicate for maximum production of the seed. Nothing much more of value to us."

"Imagine that," Frank said, obviously impressed. "All that information at your fingertips. What do you suppose farmers did before the Internet provided all this kind of information? Word of mouth, I suppose, father to son, the old-fashioned way."

Towncraft grinned, realizing that the modern age of information storage and retrieval was indeed remarkable. But he also was a little surprised Frank hadn't picked up on something obvious. He was about to announce his realization, but Brendan beat him to it.

"So I'm guessing the harvest of the onion seeds was over at the farm in my vision," he said. "And so was the drying period. The spent onions had been recently ploughed into the ground, and that's why the smell was so strong." He seemed pleased with himself, and with good reason. All of this was pure speculation, of course, but it did make sense.

Arnold grunted, a big smile on his face. "Right you are, my young agronomist, but there's an important question; one I'll wager you can't answer: Where do you suppose the farmer and his wife were? Seems likely Bryan had this young woman as a prisoner for a day or two, so who is she, and why is this farmhouse available as a place for him to do his nasty work? Do you suppose he killed other people there, besides the poor young woman?"

"Umm, that's five question, Arnold," Franks said with a grin. "Not one."

Arnold glared back at his uncle before responding irritably, "Okay. Okay, Frank. But you get my point, right?"

The questions posed by Arnold produced no direct responses from Brendan or Frank, as he predicted. They now sat deep in thought, and all three of them started to ponder these and several other ugly questions: Who was Bryan's latest victim? Where was this farm? Even more importantly, where was Bryan headed, now that he was finished using and abusing his latest victim?

One thing was abundantly clear: Bryan may well be on a rampage for revenge, bringing death to anyone who helped his brother and the police discover his whereabouts, months earlier, and maybe even anyone against whom he held a personal grudge–like his own mother–but it was also evident that he was taking time out along the way to satisfy his vile urges. This might mean he would be delayed again, sidetracked in his prime intent. The uncertainty of all this played heavily on the three collaborators as they silently dealt with their fears and pondered what they could possibly do with the meager information they now had.

Brendan also started to have one other nagging fear, about something that had not occurred to him before. What if Bryan had the same psychic abilities he had? What if he could see and hear what Brendan was doing, where he and his family now lived? Brendan realized his own experiences were a long way from anything that could be explained by science, but they had often proven reliable, if not complete. What if Bryan could channel with him, detect where he was now hiding with his family? This thought, and the implications for the added threat his insane brother presented, made Brendan shudder in horror, but he said nothing to his companions. He decided to put these thoughts out of his mind, for now.

Brendan returned to his Internet searches. He was trying to find information on where onions were grown strictly for seed. If such farms were scattered, that information would make tracking down Bryan's latest killing spot difficult. But, he reasoned, maybe onion seed farms are located in relatively small areas. That would be a lucky break. He mentioned these things to Frank, who seemed sure the police would soon find an MO commonality, if and when the victim's body was found, and maybe DNA linking the crime to Bryan Olmstead. But that could take days. Brendan was right, he knew. Coming at this from the aspect of locations where onion seeds were produced was a more sensible approach.

Frank suddenly picked up the phone. He'd decided to share their latest discoveries with Detective Segura and suggest to him that he might work on the onion seed clues. Their conversation was brief, but after hanging up Frank reported that Segura seemed dubious about the scant help he'd been given. He promised to call again the first thing next morning, however.

Later, after everyone had gone to bed, Arnold told Kathleen about the phone message from Marlie Bartholome that may have informed Bryan where Tim and his family were staying. He had toyed with the idea of saying nothing to her about this, but decided she might find out from someone else. That would not be right. Kathleen quietly wept when she was reminded of the fate of the Arcata family, and Arnold hugged her in silence, offering whatever comfort he could. When she settled a bit, she whispered, "How could a loving God allow such things to happen, Arnold?"

Arnold toyed with the idea of delivering his standard atheistic view on this subject, but he chose not to answer at all. Instead, he just squeezed her tight.

***

The next morning came and Art Segura did not call. Frank tried reaching the detective, but he was told that Segura had taken the day off. Frank, plainly peeved, tried reaching Segura's home phone and his cell, but without luck. He left messages in three places.

"That's damned annoying," he said to no one in particular.

"What is, Frank?" Arnold asked. He had been reading his morning newspaper, the Portland *Oregonian,* and had not paid much attention to what his uncle was doing.

"What? Oh, I needed to ask Segura if he's found out where onion seeds are grown. Can't get him. Seems to me, based on what we learned on the computer, that onion seeds must be grown in specific areas, as Brendan surmised. You know, places where there's the right amount of sunlight for drying, low humidity, correct soil and drainage. I was hoping Segura might have done some digging into that subject. Anything special in the news?"

"Not really. More of the same. Did you write down the name of that agronomist, or whatever he is? The professor at U.C. Davis."

"Yeah, I did." Frank thumbed through his copious notes. "Here it is: Dr. Arthur Saldovitch. Yugoslavian, maybe?"

"Sounds like. Why don't I give him a call...?" Arnold looked at the hall clock and realized it was too early. No chance that a university professor would be in his office at this time. The two men had been up for a while, but the rest of the house was still quiet. Even the two boys had not yet stirred.

They were both then startled by the phone ringing. Frank still held the cordless unit in his hand, and he responded quickly. "That'll be Art, no doubt," he said, pushing the talk button.

But it wasn't Segura, it was Tim Bartholome calling for Brendan.

"No, he's still in bed, Tim. This is Frank Dobson. What's up? Where are you?"

Frank listened for a while and then he said, "You sure it's him?"

More listening and grunting. "Have you contacted the local sheriff?"

"What's going on, Frank?" Arnold asked, now quite alarmed. *Had Bryan found the Bartholome family? Were they in danger?* He knew Brendan would want to talk to his pal, so he rushed up the stairs to awaken his guest, hoping no one else would be disturbed. But Brendan had heard the phone, was already coming down, anxious to hear of any new developments.

"It's Tim, Brendan," Towncraft said.

Frank immediately passed the phone to the younger man, still in pajamas, and he said, "When you're done, I need to talk to him again."

"Everything all right, Tim?" Brendan's anxiety was evident.

"Well, yes and no. Nothing bad has happened, exactly, but I think we may have someone following us. Can't be certain, but the same vehicle with a lone driver has been on our tail ever since we left Vegas. Stopped at the same restaurants we have each time, and he is now staying in the same motel as us. Marlie's scared to death, and so is Trish. I'm across the street right now, gassing up the car, and I'm going to bring coffee back to the room and we can hit the road real quick. No sign of the man yet, but I can see his car. I was hoping to get a good look at him. Bryan looks exactly like you, right, Bren?"

"Pretty much, yeah. But he's been known to use disguises. Where are you?"

"Just outside Mammoth Lakes, on Highway 395. We're heading north."

"Anything I can do? Have you told Detective Segura about the guy following you?

"No, I can't get him. Can't call the local sheriff because I don't have any real evidence it is Bryan. Or that he means us any harm. Could be just–"

"Where are you headed, Tim?" Brendan asked.

"No special plans. Reno, maybe; or Lake Tahoe. At least we're seeing some attractive countryside. That helps ease the misery of what's going on. You guys all okay?"

"We're fine. Listen, why not head up this way. There's a motel close by. Comfort in numbers, they say."

"We'll see. Not a bad idea, but I was hoping they would catch Bryan soon. I have to get back to work."

"Me too, pal," Brendan said with a brittle laugh. "Listen, I'll let you go. But be damned careful, man. And call again soon, okay."

Brendan seemed ready to hang up the phone, so Frank said quickly, "Ask him what kind of car this guy is driving, Brendan. And get a license plate number."

"I already got the license plate," Tim said, having heard Frank. He gave the number to Brendan and added, "The car is a late model Buick. Dark blue or maybe black. It's kinda dirty, so it's hard to tell."

## Chapter Twelve

Otis Brown, known to everyone in the June Lake area as "Echo," because of his tendency to repeat whatever anyone said to him, was mooching around behind Elton Jarvis' Ace Hardware store and lumber yard when he saw it. Otis was not the brightest bulb in the chandelier, but he knew a woman's leg when he saw one. This one, a left leg, had toenails painted bright red, a simple white flower decorating the nail of the big toe. "Oh, Jeez," he said, staggered by the sight. The leg was bare, but there were smears of blood on it. It stuck out from within a pile of scrap lumber off-cuts that Echo knew Jarvis allowed to accumulate and would donate to local poor families for their winter heat. Otis would take pieces home with him, sometimes, to fuel the fireplace in his grandmother's badly insulated little house.

"Oh, Jeez," Echo said again. He often repeated his own words as well as those of others. He toyed with the idea of trying to uncover the body, if there was a body, but decided he couldn't handle it. Scared like never before, he turned and ran. At the front of the store he ran right into Elton Jarvis, arriving for his workday.

"Hold on there, Echo," Jarvis said. "What were you doing back there?"

Echo just stood and stared, speechless, his face white as a ghost.

"Echo? You all right?" Jarvis had never seen Otis at a loss for words before, so he knew something was amiss. "What's goin' on, young feller?"

Whatever thoughts passed through Echo's feeble mind at that moment would remain unknown, for Jarvis' query went unanswered. Otis Brown, aka "Echo," leapt off the sidewalk, apparently intent on fleeing to the other side of the road, but he ran straight into the path of a loaded eighteen-wheel freight truck doing fifty miles per hour on the busy highway. The driver of the truck had no chance of stopping, and Echo's body flew high into the air before crashing to the pavement like a rejected rag doll. All nine wheels on the left side of the tractor-trailer pounded what was left of Echo, eliminating any chance the young man would survive the impact.

In ten minutes, two sheriff's vehicles and one CHP cruiser were on the scene, and then the ambulance showed up. No need for their service, really, but they hung around to deal with the mangled remains of poor Otis Brown, the dependent of his aging grandmother, Aggie Brown. Aggie was notified quickly, but she was ailing, could not make it to the site. When told that Otis was dead she reportedly said, "He was supposed to bring me some firewood."

"So tell me what you saw, Elton," Deputy Walsh said after he'd finished his examination of the scene and talked to the truck driver. "Pretty plain that this was an accident, but I have to ask all the details."

Elton Jarvis had been a resident of this area since he was a boy, and had been in the lumber business for more than twenty years. Everyone knew him well, and Deputy Bill Walsh considered him a friend. Elton told Bill what he knew, but it wasn't much. "Crazy old Echo," he said, his whole body still shaking. "I had just arrived for work, had parked my car, saw Echo looking spooked for some reason. I asked him what was up and he ran off into the road without looking. You're right, the driver of that truck never saw him until it was too late. Not his fault."

"You think maybe Echo stole something from your store?"

"Nah. That boy was not all there, but I've never known him to steal anything. He comes around here all the time, takes home scraps of wood for his grandma's fireplace. Something scared the hell out of him, it seems to me. Something real bad."

"You check around back? See if there's anything there? Not uncommon for bears to show up now and then at this time of year, and it's turning cold at night. They feel the urge to fatten up before hibernating."

"Could be, Bill. We had one by the house a few days ago. C'mon. Let's go take a look see."

The deputy checked his holstered sidearm, but he knew black bears would not normally attack two full-grown men. A cougar? Maybe?

At first they didn't see anything, and they were about to give up looking. The scrap lumber pile was at the back of the property, behind stacks of coiled fence wire. In the morning sunlight a gleaming white object suddenly caught Jarvis' eye, and he said, pointing, "What the heck is that?"

The two men rushed forward, and as they approached they could see exactly what it was. "I'll be damned," Deputy Walsh said. "C'mon, Elton," help me move some of this lumber, see if there's a whole body in here.

So the tragic accident that took the life of a young developmentally disabled man, a well-known and somewhat comic character in this friendly mountain community, was actually caused by his discovery of something that literally scared him to death.

The rest of that day was spent trying to identify the obviously young murder and rape victim. This was made especially difficult because her head had been severed, was not found anywhere. Her abdomen had multiple stab wounds. No one in the sparsely populated area had been reported missing, so there was not much to go on. There were many different tire tracks in the dirt behind Jarvis' lumber yard, contactors by the dozen driving back there each day to pick up their building materials.

That night, Elton Jarvis sat at home, still shaken from his distressing experiences, sipping on bourbon when Deputy Walsh called. There had been many phone calls throughout the day, but Elton had refused to speak to anyone. Alice Jarvis, Elton's wife of twenty-three years, asked him if he would now speak with Bill Walsh. He thought maybe he should.

"We got nothing, Elton," the deputy said soberly. "No idea who she is or where she came from. We've taken DNA–hers and the perpetrator's–but that'll take several days. Nobody in the area saw a thing last night. The coroner figures she died some time between three and four o-clock yesterday afternoon. She was not killed in your yard, he said, so the bastard probably waited until dark to put her there. What time do you lock up your gate?"

"That's just the problem, Bill. We hardly ever lock up that side gate. Never had much of a problem with theft or anything. I wish the damned thing had been locked up last night though."

"Don't you go blaming yourself, Elton. He would've found some other place to dump her body, anyway."

"Yeah, maybe so. But Echo would still be alive."

## Chapter Thirteen

When Detective Segura finally called Towncraft's house, a day later than he'd promised, he informed Frank that he had not taken a day off, as the clerk at the sheriff's office in Vista had indicated. Instead, he had been on a long road trip up the east side of the Sierra Nevada Mountains. The body of an unknown young woman had been found in a community called June Lake, mutilated in similar fashion to that of Bryan Olmstead's mother and his other recent victims, but with the added horror of decapitation this time.

"So you think it was him, Art?" Frank asked. "Any physical evidence?"

"Just DNA; but that will take a few days to analyze and match. Seems like it could be Olmstead, based on what he did to his victims. But you surely realize this kind of crime is not uncommon. We'll get some info on the size and shape of the knife real soon, maybe tomorrow. That'll be of some help. Tim Bartholome was in that area, as you know, and he says he's sure he was being followed buy someone in a black Buick, but this victim's head was severed. That's not been Olmstead's exact pattern, but he's such a crazy bastard."

"You can say that again. So Tim finally got hold of you? I assume he's all right."

"Yeah. I saw him. Spent a little time with him last night. He's okay, considering everything. Family's shook up, of course, especially after they learned about this latest victim. But there's no sign of the stalker, if that's what he was."

"Did you check out the Buick that was following him?"

"Tried to, but the numbers Tim gave me don't check out. That plate belongs on a Toyota that's sitting on a used car lot in Vegas. Been there for three weeks."

"Maybe Tim wrote down the wrong numbers. He said the car was very dirty. Did you check plates slightly different?"

"Yeah, we did. Nothing so far. But Olmstead has managed to get phony plates before, remember? He could switch plates in two minutes, and he'll no doubt switch vehicles too. I'm kinda hoping the Buick surfaces again, and soon. The California and Nevada Highway Patrols are on the lookout. Listen, I've got people checking out the onion seed thing, too. Should have something back from them in a day or so, but it sounds like a fairy story to me."

"Okay, my friend. Got anything else?"

"Nothing much. I have to get some sleep, been on the road for hours. I'll get back with you later today, or maybe first thing tomorrow."

Frank hung up the phone and found Arnold and Brendan. They were still doing work on the computer, had come up with very little new information of any value.

"There's a possible new victim, guys," Frank said, disconsolate. "In a place called June Lake. She had been stabbed to death and her head–"

"June Lake?" Brendan's face showed fear and his voice rang with alarm. "That's not far from Mammoth, where–"

"Tim's fine, Brendan," Frank said, his hand raised as if to stop Brendan thinking the worst. "Segura spent time with him last night."

"But it's the same area, Frank. This must mean that the guy in the Buick really is Bryan. He's after–"

"Don't rush to conclusions, Brendan. Like I said, Tim's fine. You have his cell phone number, right? Give him a call. Ease your mind."

"I tried already. That side of the Sierras is a bitch for cell phones. Tried several times this morning. No luck, dammit!" Brendan sat down on Arnold's desk chair and looked as if a truck had hit him. His face went white and he seemed confused.

"How far is the Mammoth area from San Diego, Brendan?" Arnold had looked up from his computer on hearing the anguish in his young friend's voice and, seeing his body language, he decided to change the subject slightly.

"It's been a while... I'd say around four hundred miles by road. Maybe more. Why do you ask?"

"And from there to here?"

"A good seven-hundred and fifty."

"And this killing took place last night, Frank?"

"Yeah. Actually, some time in the afternoon."

"And you've had no other visions or dreams, Brendan?"

"No, none since the last one at the onion farm. But I didn't see all the killings last time, if you remember, so–"

"And the body was dumped last night, Frank? Probably after dark, right?"

"Probably. So?"

"Well, it would take twenty-odd hours to drive the seven hundred-plus miles up here, even if he came directly and didn't stop to sleep or eat. But it's pretty obvious, now, that Bryan is taking his time. He's picking out victims at random, people he doesn't even know, just for the pleasure of it. Assuming, God forbid, that he kills again one more time before he comes here, or should I say goes to Brendan's house, it could be several more days. He has no idea that Brendan is with us, right"

"What's your point, Arnold?"

"Just trying to take the pressure off, that's all. There's still lots of time for the authorities to catch Bryan, so we shouldn't be so concerned."

Arnold was still in a state of deep concern himself, despite the palliative words he'd come up with, but to some degree the realization that Bryan Olmstead was taking his time seemed comforting to him somewhat. It really did give Detective Segura and the various police agencies time to catch the insane killer.

"I think the women should maybe take off somewhere, Arnold," Frank said. "This seems to be the right time for such a defensive move. Just for a few days. They should take the boys with them, of course. They wouldn't have to go far."

"What do you think, Brendan?" Arnold asked.

"I doubt if Becky would go. Makes sense, in a way, but in all honesty I'd probably be worse if they're not here with us. It feels like we're–"

"Digging in for a siege or something?" Arnold interrupted.

"Yeah. Circle the wagons." Brendan laughed nervously.

"In a way we are," Frank said. "But Arnold says there's a motel not too far away, where they could be close enough but not right here, in danger. Come to think of it, why don't you ask Tim to come up here and join us, next time he calls? His wife and daughter could also go to the same motel, stay there with the others. That way, one of us could go there each day, be with the women and children all the time, three of us waiting here or maybe going to Brendan's house. That's most likely where he'll go next, right?"

"I... I don't want to be very far away from Becky and the boys," Brendan said. He looked at his watch anxiously. "In fact, where are they now? They should have been back some time ago."

The two women and the boys were out in one of the cars, just riding around the area. The Columbia River Gorge being such a beautiful and scenic place, Kathy had decided it would be fun for the boys to see, as well as a pleasant diversion for herself and Becky. They had said they might find a quiet place for lunch, but it was now well past two o-clock, and Brendan was worried.

"They'll be here shortly," Frank said. "Don't worry. Like Arnold said, Bryan is still a long way from here, and he has no idea you are with us. So don't be anxious. Plenty of time for that a few days from now, if your brother remains loose. Anyway–"

"I hate to accept Bryan Olmstead as my brother, Frank. Even though he really is my twin." Brendan was thinking again about the possibility that Bryan could reach him on some psychic plane, and it disturbed him deeply. He was scared for himself and for his family, but he was also aware that being here he was drawing the killer to himself and his dearest friends and benefactors, the Towncrafts.

"Sorry, Brendan." Frank knew what he'd said was a mistake. "Anything new on the computer front, Arnold?"

"Not much. But I did manage to get the email address for Professor Saldovitch at UC Davis. Sent him a message a few minutes ago. I hope he'll call me soon, or reply by e-mail."

They then heard the crunch of tires in the gravel outside.

"They're here," Brendan said, and he rushed to the front door to greet his sons and his wife. The boys, bubbling with enthusiasm at what they had seen, burst into the house, anxious to show their father the pictures they had taken with Rebecca's digital camera, but Brendan ignored their pleas, was giving Rebecca a lingering hug, his relief all-too-evident.

"I'm pleased to see you too, Bren," Becky said. "But we've not been gone that long." She smiled at him warmly, searching his eyes.

"You've learned something new, haven't you?" Kathy said, reading Brendan's behavior perfectly. "What happened?"

"Bryan did it again," Brendan said, not wishing to say too much while the boys were around. They still hadn't been told the real reason for their protracted visit with "Uncle" Arnold and "Auntie" Kathleen.

"Oh, my Lord," Kathy said, unable to control her emotions fully.

"Where?" Becky asked.

"In California," Brendan said, "A place called June Lake." He added quickly, "That's a long way from here."

"Hello, weary travelers," Arnold said, emerging from his office. "Did you have fun, boys?" He was trying hard for levity, having heard every word of the exchange in the hallway. "Did I hear you say you have pictures, Jason? Come, boys, let's put 'em up on the computer for a good look. Maybe we'll print some of them."

So the two boys went with Arnold. He knew Frank and Brendan would give Kathy and Becky all the latest information. Calmly, he removed the small memory chip from Becky's camera and inserted it into his USB card reader. Soon enough the three of them were looking at the twenty-odd pictures the boys and their mother had taken; delightful pictures of the marvelous vistas along the famed Columbia River Gorge.

In the living room, Frank told the women of the slaying of a young unidentified victim in the mountain resort town of June Lake, California. "They don't know for sure that this was done by Bryan Olmstead," he added hastily, but it's a similar M.O." He made no mention of the decapitation.

Becky and Kathy both knew that Tim Bartholome and his family had been in the same area the day before, but they were quickly assured by Frank that their friends were safe.

"Have you heard from Tim today, Bren?" Becky asked, her face ashen and drawn from all she'd heard.

"Um, no. Not today. But with all the mountains around there, and where he was headed, cell phones are often useless. I tried calling him, but couldn't get through."

"So you don't actually know they are safe, do you?"

"Hey, Mom, look at this." It was Tommy. He came rushing toward his mother with a photo in his hand. "Uncle Arnold printed out the picture I took this morning."

Rebecca managed a smile and she examined the large glossy photo. She showed great enthusiasm and praised her youngest boy for his skills, but her stomach was churning with apprehension and fear. *Would this nightmare never end? What would be the next piece of bad news? Would Bryan Olmstead find them here, in this quiet corner of the world?* It was all she could do to prevent herself from crying, so deep was her concern. But she put on a brave face for the sake of her son.

Kathy was no less afraid, but she managed to put up a good front, too. "What does anyone want for dinner?" she asked cheerfully. "I should start making plans."

Frank hugged Kathy close, and he whispered, "Don't worry, Kath. Everything will be just fine, you'll see."

Kathy smiled at her friend. "Thanks, Frank," she said. "Nice try."

## Chapter Fourteen

Art Segura was at a critical point in his career. He had been a cop for more than twenty years, and a homicide detective for nearly ten. He had seen more bloody awful sights than he could count, and plenty of evidence that there are animalistic killers on the loose all the time, each with his own form of cruel insanity, each destroying the life of others and often in apparent self-satisfaction. Many times, over the years, he had toyed with the idea of changing jobs, but what would he do? He was becoming less and less able to deal with the things he saw, the indescribable horrors, and yet his options were few. This particular case was getting to him in a way he could not fully understand. Although he had tried to catch some sleep after eighteen hours on the go, he was not successful. He'd catnapped a few times, but it was daytime and the street noises outside seemed to invade his shade-drawn bedroom each time he came close to dropping into a much-needed slumber.

Suddenly the damned phone rang. "Shit!" he said, sitting up rapidly, his head pounding and his eyes burning. "Yeah," he said harshly into the phone. He reached out and flipped on the bedside light.

"Art, it's me." It was Lieutenant Jones, Segura's boss. "Did I wake you?"

Art laughed sardonically. "What do you want, Jack?"

"Some bulletins came in that you might want to take a look at. Two 1-87's, one in El Centro and another up in Oregon. Either one of them could possibly be your boy Olmstead."

One-Eighty-Seven is the universal police code number for a homicide, and Segura knew that there could be several murders in the state of California on any given night, especially in the cities. He felt sure Bryan Olmstead hadn't yet made it to Oregon, but he had enough respect for his boss, even though he disliked him, to know that he would have screened all the incoming bulletins on-line, looking for some commonality with the Olmstead killings as well as all other cases they had. That was how he spent much of his day.

"Tell me about the one in Oregon, Jack. A knife, right? I'd not chase any cases involving a gun. Not this time."

"The victim was found at a farmhouse near a place called Madras. Ever hear of it?"

"Madras, did you say?" Segura took a swig of water from the glass by his bedside. "That's in India, Jack."

"Not this one. Oregon. Jefferson County, east side of the Cascade Mountains. Actually, the killing was in a small town called Warm Springs, not far from Madras."

"Did you say Warm Springs? Sounds like a hell-of-a place to find a cold body. So what the devil's going on up there?"

"They found a young woman, badly mutilated and decapitated. Apparently somebody up there actually read the

134

bulletins, saw similarities to the Olmstead killings and sent this report in pretty quick. Write down a couple of phone numbers, will you."

"Did you say 'decapitated,' Jack?"

"Yeah, I did. I know what you're thinking. Not exactly the same MO. But don't rule it out until we get DNA or other evidence, okay."

"All right. Give me the numbers and the name of the contacts in Madras."

"The guy on the scene is a Deputy Tubbs, county of Jefferson sheriff."

Segura couldn't help laughing a little, despite his mood and fatigue. He pictured a fat uniformed deputy called "Tubbs."

"What the hell's so funny, Art?"

Jones' lack of humor was well known to everyone he worked with.

"Just give me the numbers, Jack," Segura snarled. *Surely Olmstead can't be up in Oregon yet, can he?*

Jones read him the numbers, and then he added, "I'd not overlook the one down in El Centro, Art. And are you certain he'll not use a gun? He did before, remember? I actually checked the unexplained 1-87's with a handgun as the weapon."

Bryan Olmstead had previously used a gun, had killed four young women the same way. In his recent slaughter rampage, however, he was exclusively using a knife. Segura sensed Jones had other 1-87's he'd looked into, but the majority of killings in the big cities were gang-related these days. Some would involve a knife, but there would be lots more with guns.

The victims were seldom young white women, however. Mostly they were other young men–the macho stuff or drug turf problems. "So did you have something else that's interesting?" he said.

"Maybe. A couple of young women killed with gunshots to the back of the head, execution style, small caliber. One in Gilroy and another in Oakland. You want to take a look."

"My guess is he's still knife-happy, Jack. Tell me more about the El Centro one."

"Don't have much info, yet. Multiple stab wounds, young female victim, raped and abused before being killed."

"El Centro doesn't sound likely. In the opposite direction from all of Olmstead's probable targets."

"Yeah, I know that, but he could be headed down to Mexico. Stopped on the way to indulge his sadistic tastes and is now in Ensenada or some other place way south of the border. The MO is a perfect match. Young blonde female, multiple knife wounds in the abdomen, apparent rape."

"What about the Gilroy shooting?" Segura knew that Gilroy was in Northern California, the direction he assumed Olmstead was headed.

"An older woman than the others. Late thirties, early forties. Raped, shot with a small caliber pistol, probably a twenty-two, and dumped in a ravine. Similar story in Oakland; could be the same perp."

Segura grunted, still thinking mostly about the other 1-87's, the ones where the victim was knifed. "Bryan doesn't go for older women, Jack, except in revenge. For his sadistic pleasures he seems to like them much younger. But I'll take a close look at El Centro when I come in. The one in Oregon sounds more likely, and it sounds like he's getting close to... I expect Olmstead's brother is his prime target. He may well have learned where Brendan lives from the Arcatas. You realize that, right?"

"If you're still angling for a trip to Oregon, Detective, the answer is still negative. I wouldn't want the Carlsons to be the next victims anymore than you do, so if the Madras killing turns out to be your boy I'll maybe change my mind. But you don't yet know if Olmstead had anything to do with the June Lake killing. In fact, you have no idea where he is or which way he's headed, do you?"

Segura acknowledged these sorry truths and he hung up. He had twice asked his boss for approval to go up to join the ultimate potential victims of Bryan Olmstead in Oregon, where they all seemed to be sitting like live bait in a trap, and still he'd been denied. He sat on the edge of his bed, scratching absently at his chest, staring at the information he'd scribbled on his notepad. He always seemed to get a flare-up of eczema whenever he got tired and tense, and he sure as hell was both right now. He downed the rest of the tepid water and groaned, realizing any chance of catching some shut-eye was now long gone. He knew he should check the details of the Oregon 1-87, and maybe all the others Jones had mentioned, too, but first he needed a shower and a shave. Then, he'd find something to eat. He knew his body had been abused lately, and this promised to be another hellish day.

\*\*\*

137

By the time Segura made contact with Deputy Tubbs, in Madras, after a brief and virtually fruitless conversation with the Jefferson County Sheriff himself, Tubbs had something new to report. Not much value to Segura, but it seemed immensely satisfying to Tubbs:

"Yes sir, Detective," he said. "We found that little girl's automobile less than two hours after the body was found. A Honda Civic, and I just had a hunch. I said to my–"

"Deputy, were you able to get fingerprints off the car? Somebody must've dumped it after abducting the girl. Either that or she drove it to where you found it and jumped into another vehicle right there; probably the killer's. And what about the crime scene itself?"

"No luck on both counts. The Honda had been cleaned pretty well of fingerprints, and so had the farmhouse where we found the body. We're doing fiber analysis, of course, but I'm afraid–"

"Farmhouse, huh? Anybody in the area see a stranger? Driving a Buick, maybe?"

Segura knew his last question made little sense. The notion that Olmstead was driving a Buick was flimsy at best, and anyway, he wouldn't have had time to drive all the way up to central Oregon since Tim Bartholome saw the last of the Buick that had been following him. If it really was a Buick, and if it really had been following him.

"Strangers pass through here all the time, Detective. And a Buick is not exactly an exotic or rare breed, now is it?"

Segura grunted. Tubbs was right. "You got DNA, right?"

"Yes, sir. I was just about to tell you that. We'll get the report back from the lab in six or seven days."

"Christ! Can't you get the results any sooner than that?"

"Not as a rule. We can get the mitochondrial DNA a day or two sooner, maybe, but that won't be of much use to you, will it? You're anxious to compare with what we have with Olmstead's, no doubt. Is he known to be up this way?"

"We don't know where the hell he is, but we think he likely has other targets in Oregon, north of where you are, so tell the labs to put a priority on this, okay? And call me if anything new comes up. I mean anything. You got my numbers, right?" He was surprised that Tubbs understood the important difference between DNA types.

Segura sighed as he hung up, and he scratched some more. Then he went to his den and found a map of the Western United States. He examined the state of Oregon, unsure where The Dalles was located. Pretty soon he found it, and then, to his horror, he located Madras. *Holy Shit!* Madras was no more than seventy or eighty miles south of where Brendan Carlson and his family were holed up with the Towncrafts and Frank Dobson. Should he tell Frank and Arnold about this latest discovery? No real way of ruling Olmstead out as the killer in Madras, not soon anyway. But if it was not him, then alarming the folks at the Towncraft house would be unkind and unproductive. So he decided to say nothing to them at this point. He poured another cup of black coffee, lit up a cigar and started reviewing his notes. Surely to Christ there would be a breakthrough soon. The Highway Patrol or the cops in Reno finding the Buick, maybe?

Or some other lucky break? He needed something that would confirm or deny that Olmstead had killed one of these latest victims. Or maybe neither! This startling realization jolted Segura. Yeah, maybe Olmstead had nothing to do with either of these latest killings. If that was the case, then where the hell was the crazy bastard? El Centro? Gilroy? He decided to try reaching Tim Bartholome, hoping there was no new bad news on that front.

## Chapter Fifteen

"I told you we should have brought the Buick, Chuck."

"Yeah, yeah, smart ass. But it's a little too late for that now, don't you think? Anyway, there wasn't room in your piddling little trunk for all the damned luggage the women brought along with 'em. Besides, what makes you think the asshole that done this wouldn't have just loved to get at your fancy new car?"

"It has an alarm system, Chuck. Something you should think about getting for this old battleship."

Sam grunted and sat in the drivers seat, the door wide open. The two friends, Chuck Albright and Martin Scappelli, were alongside Chuck's aging Chevy Suburban, located in the public parking facility across from the cruise ship docks in downtown San Diego. They had come back from their Mexican Riviera cruise to find the vehicle vandalized, all four tires slashed, the sides of the car scratched badly and the radio antenna snapped off. Their wives had been dispatched to a nearby restaurant to drink coffee and wait while the two men dealt with the police, who had spent little time on the problem and had left the site already, admitting there wasn't much they could do. The parking lot manager had also come by to take a brief look, but he'd insisted his company had no liability.

"Check your ticket," he had said to them, and Chuck knew he was right.

"I called Triple-A for you. They said they'll have somebody here shortly."

So now they were alone, waiting, with Martin regretting he'd not brought his cell phone with him, as well as his own car.

Four hours later, after more hassles, they were on the highway bound for Barstow, Chuck and Muriel's home. Chuck had coughed up over eight hundred dollars for a new set of tires, and he was not a happy man.

"But we did have a nice cruise, honey," Muriel said after a long icy period. "It's too bad about the tires, but you have to admit they were a long way from new, and this car is long overdue for a paint job." She was struggling, trying to find a way to console her angry husband.

They had intended to head up to Bakersfield for a few days, after the cruise, to visit with Muriel's sister. But this setback had soured Chuck's taste for such a visit. Muriel didn't argue with him, knowing it would only make matters worse. They drove on in silence for a bit; not even a radio to help release the tension.

"Well, I'll be happy to get home," Martin said. "There's a lot of chores I've been putting off for some time."

"You'll stay overnight though, won't you?" Muriel said. "It'll be dark before we get to our place, and then you've got what, a five-hour drive to Flagstaff."

"More than six," Martin said. "But I think we'll just pick up our car and get right back on the road. That okay with you, Jane?"

Jane Scappelli was unsure what to say. She was an old school chum of Muriel, and that was the bond between these two retired couples. She really was disappointed that they were not going to Bakersfield. Muriel's sister was also her friend; one she didn't see often enough. But she knew Martin had made up his mind.

The subject was dropped, and the four rode on in silence, their brief but enjoyable holiday spoiled by the unfortunate intrusion on their lives by a petty street vandal. Little did they know that a much more dangerous criminal had impacted their happy return. After three more hours on the road they faced their second major setback in an unhappy day. The Albright home had been broken into, a few items stolen, including some cash, and the Scappelli's new Buick had been taken from the garage.

"What in the hell is this world coming to?" Chuck Albright said, visibly shaken. "Judas, Priest! What in God's name have we done to deserve this shit?"

Muriel was in tears, and Jane Scappelli attempted to console her friend. "It's not so bad, honey," she said. "Better he broke in while we were away. If you'd been home, no telling what might have happened. And as far as the car is concerned, it has On-Star, so they'll be able to track it down in no time."

They had called the police already, and Martin was now busy on the phone, trying to find the On-Star customer service number. He overheard his wife's comments and threw a little

143

cold water on her optimistic statement. "I can't find the damned phone number, Jane. You sure you didn't write it down in your little book? I gave it to you the day we picked up the car. Then there was that little card the company mailed us, a few days later, remember?"

"No, sweetie, I'm sorry. I sure don't remember you giving me a number, or a card, nothing like that."

Martin was exasperated. The phone company had not been able to give him a number either, because he didn't even have a town where On-Star headquarters were located. The operator admitted she knew the name "On-Star," but she thought it was something to do with cable television.

"Bert has a new Cadillac," Chuck said, snatching the phone from his friend's hand. "That'll have On-Star, for sure. Let me give him a call."

In a matter of minutes Chuck had obtained from another friend the phone number to call at On-Star and Martin, still exasperated, made the call and informed them of the theft of his Buick. For several seconds during the call his mind went blank trying to think of his account pass code, but he finally remembered.

"Okay, Mr. Scappelli, we will trace the car right away and get the information to the police. Don't you worry, it will not take very long. Give me a phone number where you can be reached." Martin had always found the On-Star people so friendly and anxious to please; but he'd only ever contacted them from within the car, where the number was not needed.

So the Scappelli's decision to go straight home without an overnight stay at the Allbright's house was academic. They could have rented a car, certainly, but they decided to stay the night in Bakersfield anyway. After the police had been to the house, taken statements and dusted for fingerprints, the four friends spent the rest of the evening drowning their sorrows in bourbon. After several drinks, even the irascible old Chuck finally calmed down. They actually ended up laughing about the unlikely coincidences that had befallen them. And when they went to bed they all slept well, despite their plight.

The next morning, at a few minutes before seven, Chuck was awakened by the phone at his bedside. It was the Barstow police.

"Mr. Albright," the sergeant said, "tell your friend that On-Star located the Buick. It's in Visalia. The Tulare County Sheriff has a patrol vehicle on the way to the site as we speak."

"That's good news, Sergeant," Chuck said. "And the guy who stole it?"

"We don't know anything more, yet, except that the vehicle has been stationary overnight, maybe for a day or two. It has undoubtedly been abandoned. We'll get back to you when we have more information. Oh, I almost forgot. On-Star tells us there's a phone comes with that unit. Ask your friend to give me that number, we need to see if the thief used it to call anyone."

Sam had to wake Martin to obtain his On-Star phone number and after more confusion, with Martin searching through his wallet, they gave it to the officer, but the also added the number for a separate cell phone that was also in the vehicle when it was stolen.

## Chapter Sixteen

Bryan Olmstead was having the time of his life. He was in a constant state of arousal over the things he had been doing and the big plans he'd made. He had outsmarted the police for several days now, in fact he felt sure his evasive tactics were completely effective. And he had taken his cruel pleasures here and there on his leisurely way north for the ultimate experience, a satisfying confrontation with his brother and family.

He had found another library, was searching for information that would help him complete his mission. Libraries had been useful to him often before, and his skills on the computer almost always produced good results. This time his disguise was more dramatic than before, and much easier to deal with: he'd shaved his head. He had done this once as a teenager, in a form of adolescent self-expression that produced derision from his mother. She had laughed at him so hard she spilled her damned drink all down a new dress, which was a rare luxury for her. Angry at this outcome, and without warning, she had thrown the glass at Bryan, hitting him right on top of his unprotected skull. He had ducked, but not fast enough to avoid the missile. Eighteen stitches it had taken to patch up the cuts, and he was left with two ugly scars. He fingered these scars often, and he thought of his mother's drunken rage as he did so now, seated at a computer in the Redding public library. "But that depraved bitch is now in hell," he muttered with venom. "How does it feel, Ma? Hot enough for you?"

He looked around self-consciously, realizing he'd spoken these words aloud. Nobody had heard him, apparently, so he continued with his search on the computer. He wiped the drool from his chin and then rubbed his hand on his cotton t-shirt. It was hot, and the air conditioning system seemed to be ineffective. But he concentrated, working with an on-line telephone directory. He knew that Brendan lived in the Greater Portland area, in Oregon. That much he had learned from the sad little Arcata father who lived in Brendan's former home in Rancho Bernardo. Bryan giggled as he thought of this man, one of his four victims in that house. *The son-of a bitch was not living there now. Not living anywhere!*

Soon, he had what he was looking for. *Aaah, here he is, Brendan J. Carlson, my darling brother. This is so damned easy!* Grinning with satisfaction, he wrote down the address and the phone number. Then he logged on to Mapquest.com and, minutes later, armed with all the information he needed, he logged off, shut down the computer and walked outside into the relatively quiet main street of Redding. He climbed into the stolen Mazda pickup truck, on which he had already switched license plates twice, and reached for the cell phone he'd stolen with the fancy Buick Lucerne, days before. He hadn't used this phone yet, was saving it for his last crucial moves. He was now ready to make an assault on his ultimate target, and he imagined he could smell the blood of his brother and other smells, much more provocative odors from Brendan's wife. What was her name? He couldn't remember. He had learned her name from Maria Arcata, days before, but hadn't written it down. That little detail would soon be recouped, however. And no matter what her name, she would provide him with sweet pleasures of several different kinds. Brendan would be a witness to it all, of course, and then they would both die a painful death. He dialed the number as he reached for his crotch and rubbed his growing erection.

Bryan felt smug about all he had accomplished so far. He had planned most of his various moves to confuse the police. He knew they were onto him, so he had to be clever. He felt sure he had plenty of time to do what he really wanted, and even some time for side-trips, a little entertainment here and there along the way.

After four rings, Bryan heard the message machine click on and a child's voice said, "Carlson residence. We're not home, so leave a message. If you're calling for Brendan, he can be reached at his office, two-two-six, six-six-three-one." Bryan smiled. It was all so damned easy. He checked his wristwatch, a nice Seiko stolen from the same house he had picked up his most recent vehicle. It was just after four o'clock, so Brendan would likely still be at work. He put down the phone and started to think, to make his plans for the final phases of his approach to the place his brother was hiding. And then he saw her, the lithe and lovely girl walking back to her car, tossing her blonde mane provocatively. "Well, well, well," he said aloud. "What delicious treat do we have here? Brendan, my brother, you'll have to wait a day or two, while I play a little game with my new friend." He followed the girl's Toyota Prius out of the parking lot, still rubbing himself in anticipation. He was sure this one was another college co-ed; he loved making these smart-ass little girls realize they were totally subservient to him, and ultimately worthless. Brendan wasn't going anywhere, could certainly wait a few more days.

***

Segura decided he'd better tell Frank about the murder near Madras after all. It would be days before DNA evidence showed proof of Bryan's guilt on this one, or perhaps his innocence, but Frank really should know about it, though he would suggest withholding the information from the others. He picked up his phone and started pushing buttons, but then he suddenly thought of something. *What in the hell is wrong with me?* He disconnected and started over, this time dialing the number for Deputy Tubbs, in Oregon.

His conversation was direct and to the point:

"It's Art Segura again, Deputy. Sorry to interrupt your work, but there's one question I should have asked you before. Was the farm where the girl was killed an onion farm, by any chance?"

There was a long silence, and then Tubbs said, incredulous, "Now what in the hell gave you that idea, Detective? Did I say anything about onions? The sheriff, perhaps?"

"No, you didn't and he didn't. So tell me, was it an onion farm?"

"Onion seed farm."

"What?"

"The Serbeins grow onions for seed. Is that important?"

"It could well be very damned important, Deputy. Onion seeds are produced when the onion itself is allowed to remain in the ground, right? After the seeds are harvested the onions begin to rot and smell bad, is that it?"

"Oh, yeah. At this time of year, when the wind is just right, I can smell them all the way to my house, which is seventeen miles–"

"Great. Just what I wanted to hear. Be sure to let me know as soon as you get DNA, or anything on the knife that was used, fiber evidence or anything, okay?"

"Sure will, sir."

"You mentioned the name of the people who own the farm. Are they all right?"

"The Serbeins? Yeah, they're fine. Shocked as hell, of course, but they were away at the time of the murder, visiting family."

Segura muttered a sort of prayer, knowing what might have happened to another innocent and unconnected family, had they been home. "Freaky chances," he said.

"I didn't quite catch that, Detective."

"Oh, nothing. Just contemplating the way life sometimes deals people strange cards. Thanks, Deputy. I'll get back to you in a few days."

Segura hung up and again hesitated about calling Frank Dobson with what he now knew. Things were not looking good, and there was no time to waste. Better that Frank and Arnold should know of the threat they seemed to be facing, now that it seemed certain Bryan Olmstead was within a few miles of Towncraft's home. Better yet that he actually get off his ass and go join Frank and Arnold. *How, in God's name, did Olmstead know where the old professor lived? Did he also know that his brother and his family were holed up in the Towncraft home?* He decided to make the call.

* * *

Frank Dobson knew he was in trouble. He felt a tightness in his chest that he'd been anticipating for some time; his doctors had cautioned him to be alert to such a change. His health had been compromised dramatically by the early symptoms of a condition called ALS, a progressive disease he knew would slowly kill him; and yet he had told no one, not even his wife, Hilda. His doctor had also told him there would be long periods free from the symptoms of this incurable disease, in the early stages. But soon, in addition to the painful leg problems, cramps and associated twitching he had already experienced, he would inevitably start to have difficulty breathing. He had already noticed minor breathing troubles on occasions, and he knew these would gradually get more severe. Ultimately, all this would lead to swallowing difficulties and then the inability to speak. In the terminal stages, maybe two or three years down the road, if he was lucky, he would need to be hospitalized, fed intravenously and sustained by mechanical devices of all kinds. He had already completed a living will, in which he had stipulated "no heroic measures," but he had this stashed away in a safety deposit box in

Pittsburgh. He'd made up his mind that he was going to tell Arnold all about these dread facts when he felt his chest tighten, and he wondered if this was the tense situation he and his friends were in, or maybe it was the beginning of the next stage in his battle with what most people know as Lou Gherig's Disease.

Arnold had seen some of his uncle's discomfort, and had previously wondered what it could be, the obvious leg cramps and other fidgeting. He decided to ask, hoping to hear that it was nothing significant. He slowly came to realize that it was significant and then some.

So Frank started to tell what he knew of his illness, using euphemisms and partial truths. Arnold sat in stony silence for a few seconds, and when Frank had said all he intended to, Arnold felt incredibly powerful emotions flood through him. Then the phone rang. Frank took the call, it was Segura. Frank's face and his responses revealed very little during the brief conversation, he was simply grunting most of the time. He thanked the detective and hung up.

Arnold had been distracted anyway, was dwelling on what Frank had told him When the phone call ended, realizing just how much Frank's revelation had added to his existing anxiety, he stood up and said sternly, "That settles it then. We are all going to leave this place. I mean all of us. We need to get you to the Mayo Clinic, in Minnesota. There, they have the finest of clinicians, and if anyone can help you, they are the most likely ones. The rest of us will go there to be with you and to be safe. Olmstead will not find us here, and he'll move on. He is not likely to follow us all the way to Minnesota. Anyway, it sounds as if Segura has got a–"

"It's incurable, Arnold," Frank said, shaking his head. "There's nothing anyone can do, not even at the Mayo. Besides, there's no sense us all–"

"There must be something they can do. I'll bet there are new medications, maybe some clinical trials you can get involved with." Arnold was now up and pacing, plainly distraught. Not so much at the impending threat from Bryan Olmstead–and that surprised him–but at what he'd learned about his uncle's health. He had grown to love this man dearly, and he was not about to allow him to die without doing everything he could to help. He would use his substantial wealth to make sure Frank got every possible chance.

"I'm already in one, Arnold."

"What?"

"I'm already in a clinical trial. Taking a medication called Myotrophin. It's supposed to slow down the progression, but it'll not cure me. I also take Xanax, to control the leg twitching."

"Xanax? I thought you said–"

"Yeah, well, I lied. I'm not afraid of flying; you know that. I just said I was because, well, I didn't want you and Kathy worrying. You'll not tell her, right?"

"If that's what you want, no. You've told Hilda?"

Frank paused, eying his nephew oddly. "No, I haven't," he said. "She'll find out soon enough; but not yet."

Things went totally quiet between them for a while, each man deep in thought. Then, suddenly, Arnold said, "You have any idea about how much I care for you, Frank? I mean, what you've told me is the worst thing..."

Frank stood up and grinned. "No, not in so many words. But sometimes words aren't needed. And it's mutual."

They embraced each other in silence for a while, and it was then that Kathy came into the den. She had been into the garden with Rebecca and the two boys, picking some flowers and homegrown vegetables. Brendan had gone to check out the Riverside Motel, a few miles up the gorge; had been gone for a while.

"Well, aren't we showing affection?" Kathy said lightly. And then, more seriously, she said, "What's happened? You know something new, don't you? It's not Tim and Trish, is it? Please tell me it's not–"

Arnold quickly put Kathy's mind at ease. "No, darling," he said. "That's not it. So far as we know the Bartholomes are fine. But there is news about Bryan Olmstead." He looked at Frank, who nodded and picked up the cue.

"He may be in Oregon already, Kath. The police aren't sure it was him, but there was a killing in a place near Madras, a couple of hours south of here. Segura's checking, and they hope to have proof of Bryan's involvement soon, one way or another."

Kathy had not been told much about Brendan's latest visions, so she knew very little about the details he'd conveyed from the vision of Bryan's cruel slaughter of a young woman in a farmhouse not far away. Arnold began to tell her these details now, and she sat down, her face drawn in anguish. She was totally silent as she listened, and when he'd finished she seemed deeply shocked, but she was also perplexed.

"How can that happen, Arnold? I mean... can that kind of psychic experience even include smells? How is that possible?"

Frank said, "It's entirely possible, Kath. The senses we ordinarily experience are all processes of the brain, after all. The receptors for odors are the olfactory nerves, but the brain is the actual organ of all the senses. If psychic transference of visual experiences are possible, and they seem to be–in a small number of people–then any of the other senses can also be involved. I once had a case where–"

"Did you say the farm where this latest one... is it an onion farm?"

Frank shook his head. "We don't know that yet. Segura will probably–"

"Where is Brendan now?" Kathy said, suddenly aware that their young friend was not with her husband and Frank.

"Yeah, where is my dad?" It was Jason, who had been in the bathroom with his brother and his mother, washing their hands after their adventure in the garden. He had heard Kathy's question.

"He's gone down the road, to the store," Arnold said quickly. "We needed some supplies and more soda-pop. You guys are drinking it so fast we ran out."

"Soda-pop?"

Arnold realized this was an anachronistic term, and his age was showing. He grinned. "Coke," he said. "Coke and other fizzy drinks were all called soda-pop not so long ago. Aaah, here's your mother and brother. Rebecca, you know what soda-pop is, right?"

Rebecca looked puzzled, having sensed a tension in the air that seemed entirely unrelated to the lighthearted subject of soft drinks. But she played along anyway:

"Oh, yeah," she said. "Coke and such. Hey, boys, did you tell Arnold about the weasel?"

They had spotted a weasel in the yard, and although the boys had seen them in the zoo, finding one here, in the wild, was a great thrill for them.

Arnold laughed. "We call him Charlie," he said. "He's actually quite a friendly little fellow, but I wouldn't get too close to him, if I were you. They can bite you know, and I also suspect Charlie has fleas."

At that moment they heard Brendan's car return, and Arnold eyed Frank. "Come on, Frank," he said, winking. "Let's go out and help Brendan bring in the soda-pop."

"Can I come too?" Jason asked.

"We can handle it," Arnold said quickly. "I think Auntie Kathleen wants you to help her in the kitchen. Right, sweetheart?"

Kathleen was still partly in shock, but she realized that Frank and Arnold needed to bring Brendan up to date about Bryan's latest evil. She said, "Yeah, come on guys, both of you can help me shuck some fresh corn."

"Shuck?" Jason made a funny face. "First it's Soda-Pop, now it's something called shuck?"

Tommy cuffed Jason up the back of his head and pushed him toward the kitchen. "Come on, moron," he said. "You got a lot to learn."

"Don't try to kid me that you knew these words," Jason said. "Cuz I'm not buying it, kid."

Frank watched them go, and then he said to their grinning mother, "Go ahead, Rebecca. Help them in the kitchen. Arnold and I will bring the stuff in from the car."

Frank seemed resolute, so Arnold agreed, though he knew there was little to carry.

"Bryan's in Oregon," Frank said when they were outside with Brendan. "He was less than a hundred miles away from here two days ago."

"Two days?" Brendan showed alarm. How can that be, Frank? He was in June Lake two days ago, wasn't he?"

"Frank, what are you saying?" Arnold's face showed his puzzlement. "You just said–"

"I know what I said. I didn't want Kathy alarmed, so I lied. That call from Segura, that's what he told me. You seemed interested in other things when I hung up, and then Kathy came in." He turned to Brendan. "This probably means the June Lake killer was not Bryan."

"So he killed again? Somewhere near here? And it was an onion farm?"

"Yeah. That's what Segura thinks. Come on, open up the trunk. Let's not say anything about this to Kathy and Rebecca, okay?"

## Chapter Seventeen

Art Segura was agitated. He had in front of him a list of all the automobiles stolen in California within a seven-day window following the murder of Bryan Olmstead's mother, in Arizona. He also had his well-used map of the Western United States. The list of stolen automobiles was long, but there were not many incidents in rural areas, and very few were Buicks. He had highlighted the latter, five of them; but he hadn't really needed to. The only stolen Buick that seemed important was the one taken from a private home in Barstow; but on closer inspection of the details of this theft there was a problem. The theft had been reported two days *after* Tim Bartholome had told him he was being followed by a Buick. This notwithstanding, the vehicle had been found in Visalia, a location that fit reasonably well with what Segura presumed would be Olmstead's intended direction and his ultimate goal: to end up in Oregon.

Segura knew coincidences often prevented logical conclusions, and more than once he had let a suspect slip away by following a false lead. He didn't intend that to happen in this case. Way too much at stake. He picked up the phone and called the number for the jurisdiction that had been involved in the case of the stolen 2005 Buick Lucerne, a brand-new car, a model new to the brand. After identifying himself to the desk sergeant at the Barstow Police headquarters he was given the information he needed: The day the vehicle was stolen was not known, the owner having been away from the Buick for seven days, on a cruise somewhere, so the car could have been stolen several days before the owner discovered the loss. So that erased one of Segura's concerns.

"I presume you checked the vehicle for fingerprints, Sergeant?"

"We did, and so did the CHP in Fresno. A few small partials were found, nothing useable."

"The information I have says the car was found the day after it was reported stolen, is that right? Pretty quick work by somebody."

"Right, Detective, but like I said, it was probably stolen several days before the owner knew it. The Buick had On-Star, making it asy to track, and the driver himself probably had no idea it was even on the vehicle. You're familiar with On-Star, right?"

"What? Yeah, somewhat." Segura was ready to hang up, so he said, "I'm very grateful to you, Sergeant, and if you get–"

"Before you go, there's one other thing. There was a cell phone stolen with the Buick. It was not recovered with the car."

"Why would someone with On-Star need a cell phone as well?"

"I guess the mobile phone can be carried and used when you're not in the vehicle. The On-Star phone is only usable in the car."

"Yeah, I suppose you're right."

Segura couldn't believe his good fortune. He knew that a cell phone was a small radio transmitter. Same thing with the On-Star phone. When used to make a call, it can be roughly located by triangulation between the cell transmission towers. The fact that the thief had kept the mobile phone was of huge potential value. He would need a court order to get the details of all calls made from this phone since it was stolen, but that would be easy. "Give me that cell number, Sarge," he said. "And I need the name of the mobile service company, as well as the name on the account."

He had to work fast. If, as he suspected, Bryan Olmstead had already made his way to Oregon, he needed to know exactly where he was located, which direction he was moving, and without delay. It was quite obvious who the maniac's ultimate targets were, but could he possibly have found out where Brendan and his family were holed up already? He called Jack Jones right away. Maybe this latest development would get him a ticket on a plane to Portland? At the very least he needed fast access to the phone company technicians. They would track down the stolen mobile phone Bryan Olmstead had in his possession. Jones could handle that assignment.

But Lieutenant Jones was still not convinced. He did agree to persuade the DA to get a court order for access to the phone records on the stolen cell phone, but he wanted Segura to simply inform the various agencies in Oregon, let them handle Olmstead's threats in their own areas of responsibility.

"Look, Jack," Segura said, obviously agitated, "you and I both know the police in Oregon will do very little unless we have hard evidence of a crime committed in their jurisdiction. They have a homicide to deal with, but they have no evidence our boy is involved, so why would they care about the folks at Towncraft's House. But we should care. I know Frank Dobson is armed, okay–and he was a former cop who knows what he's doing–but he's an old man. Do you want the next news we hear to be the death of all those people now holed up in Arnold Towncraft's house?"

"Like I said before, Art, and you know it's true, we don't know for sure where Olmstead is right now. Get me some proof that he's anywhere near Towncraft's home and I'll give you the green light. Meanwhile, work closely with the cell phone company and wait for DNA match-ups on the 1-87's you think Olmstead might be involved in; Oregon or elsewhere. My guess is he's long gone. To Mexico, likely."

Segura was so mad he hung up without another word. He started pacing angrily, feeling a growing sense of frustration. He knew, on one level, that Jones was right; there was no hard evidence that Bryan Olmstead had killed anyone other than his own mother, the two sisters in Julian and the Arcata family. But he sensed that he was right despite these uncertainties. Olmstead was a crazy bastard, filled with hatred for anyone who helped bring him in last time and he would kill anyone who got in his way.

The disconsolate detective was about to pick up the phone again when it rang anyway, startling him. He hesitated, wondering if maybe Jones was calling him back to reaffirm his last edict, or maybe he had changed his mind? He decided to wait, let it ring and the answering machine would pick up. After four rings, and after his recorded outgoing message, he heard a voice he didn't recognize say words that reminded him of an avenue of investigation that he'd all but forgotten about. In fact he had regarded it scornfully: the onion smell Brendan had experienced in his vision.

"Detective Segura, this is Professor Arthur Saldovitch of UC Davis. I am an agronomist, and I have some infor–"

"Yes, Professor," Segura said, picking up the handset. "This is about onions, no doubt?"

"Yes, Detective. Someone from your department asked me to call you with the answer to a question she felt might be of value in a homicide case you're working. She could have given you this information herself, I suppose, but she assumed you might have other questions."

"Okay, so what do you have to tell me about onion farms?"

"Well, onions are grown all over the place. As for onion seed, they are produced in several places, but there are heavy concentrations of farms that specialize in the Salinas Valley, south of San Jose. There are even some close to Soledad, though much of that area is highly productive artichoke and garlic, not onions or onion seeds. There are also a few very productive seed farms in Jefferson County, in Oregon. The air there, on the east side of the Cascades, is dry, ideal for–"

"Did you say Jefferson County?" Segura's mind was racing, trying hard to make sense of what he was hearing. "And Salinas? That's near Gilroy, right?"

"Yes, it is. But an area twenty miles south of Gilroy is where the onion seed producers are concentrated. Is this of some value to you?"

Segura paused. "Well, it could be. Do you happen to have a list of farmers, or cooperatives, associations, or whatever groups these people belong to. I need names and phone numbers for California and for Oregon."

"I thought you might, and yes, I do have some information, but not much. You could call the California Department of Agriculture, and the same agency in Oregon. By an odd coincidence, however, I did some consulting with a co-op in Oregon. I have the name of their manager, George Gelson, and I have his phone number, if that would be of value. He's in Madras. That's the county seat."

"Madras? Oh, yeah. I believe it might be exactly what I need."

Though highly skeptical about Brendan Carlson's dreams and visions, Segura knew that on prior occasions they had proven helpful, so he eagerly took the information from the professor and thanked him. He disconnected and immediately called the number he'd been given for George Gelson. In minutes, he was able to confirm that among the handful of independent farmers belonging to the Jefferson County Farm Cooperative was a Henry

Serbein. Feeling as if he now had the breakthrough he needed, he confirmed this name from his notes, and yes, sure enough, this was the farmer whose home had been the killing site for the young woman in Warm Springs.

"Well I'll be damned," Segura said after this revelation. He punched his speed dial button number one, realizing how pathetic his life was. The number one button on his home phone was for his boss. *I have to get out of this job!*

But still Jones was not sold by what he heard. "No real change, Art. There's still no proof Olmstead had anything to do with the killing in Madras. And until you–"

"Jack, get real, for God's sake! Four days ago Olmstead's brother envisioned Bryan killing a young woman at an onion farm. The Serbein farm, in Jefferson County, produces onions, and there was a knifing victim found there four days ago, a young woman, and by all accounts an attractive young woman, just like Olmstead's earlier victims. I know this is not absolute proof of anything, but it is one hell of a coincidence, don't you think? Furthermore, Madras is less than seventy miles south of where Olmstead's brother and family are hiding. What more proof do you want? Come on, Jack!"

Jones laughed. "You're starting to sound irrational, Art. You want me to take action on the basis of a psychic experience that–"

"Brendan Carlson's psychic experiences helped lead us to this maniac's arrest the first time around, remember. So why not this time? Look, I'm going up there whether you say so or not. You can fire me, demote me, do whatever the hell you want to me, but I'm going to Oregon. I'll use my own money. We'll both be sorry of I don't go and the worst happens." Segura hung up feeling remarkably calm despite what he'd said and the implications of what he was doing. In some strange way he really did hope Jones would fire him for insubordination. He knew his file was filled with reports on his tendency to ignore direct orders, and he'd been admonished and warned several times, so it would probably fly. He had a good arrest record, though, and that had prevented severe punitive action. But if he was actually fired now, it would make a big decision for him; one he seemed reluctant to make on his own but a decision on which he had all but made up his mind. And yet... what would he do if he were not a cop? He decided to shelve this question and began to search his hell-hole of a closet for the phone book. He needed the numbers for airlines that serviced the San Diego/Portland route. Minutes later, with the wreckage of his search scattered across the worn-out carpet of his living room floor, he was booked on an Alaska Airlines flight leaving at 8:00 p.m. That would give him time to pack a bag and get to the airport, where he'd grab a burger or something. It would also give him a little time to make several more important phone calls. He had much work to do.

It would have surprised Art Segura to know that Jack Jones sat at his desk smiling for several minutes after their heated conversation. The lieutenant was a good cop, but a relentless bureaucrat. He knew that he could not justify sending an officer out of jurisdiction on something so flimsy as a psychic experience. He also knew it would be a day or two more before they would have DNA match-ups for the two killings Segura assumed were done by Olmstead, in June Lake and near Madras, Oregon, and he was as concerned as Segura himself about Brendan Carlson, his family and his friends. Furthermore, he knew that his counterpart in Wasco County, Oregon, could do little to protect them in advance of specific information. On that, Segura had been right. The Wasco County Sheriff had agreed to send a patrol car by the Towncraft home once a day, but Jones knew that was of limited value. So after his heated conversation with Segura, he sat back and smiled. "About time, Art," he muttered. "What took you so long?" He then picked up the phone and started returning the calls that had accumulated in a typical day for a watch commander in the San Diego County Sheriff's office.

## Chapter Eighteen

Arnold Towncraft didn't sleep well that night, and he really hadn't expected to. The tensions had been building steadily with each passing day, and he felt a profound sense of responsibility for the welfare of his friends, all the guests in his house. *Did he do the right thing in bringing them here?* Overriding these fears and uncertainties, all of which were oppressive enough, was the dreadful news he'd learned about Frank's health. He had grown to love his uncle dearly, after years of foolish estrangement, and the two men had been so happy whenever together, working at solving crimes that often seemed to baffle the police. Arnold had been trying for several years to get Frank and Hilda to move nearby. He knew they had both grown to hate the cold winters of central Pennsylvania, and they seemed interested enough, but had not taken action. Now, learning of Frank's inevitable demise had hit Arnold hard, and he felt a strong compulsion to intervene directly.

Arnold had not had much time alone with his uncle after the dreadful disclosure of Frank's illness, and there were many questions he needed to ask, much research he wanted to do, but he had gone to bed knowing these would have to keep. There were other matters weighing heavily on his consciousness, too. The next morning, after an early breakfast, he'd planned for Brendan to take his family, along with Kathleen, to the Riverside Motel, where they would be relatively safe. He and Frank had tried to bully Brendan into going with them, knowing Brendan would not be comfortable apart from his family. But Brendan's mixed emotions on the matter had been all too evident, and he'd finally declined, saying he felt sure Bryan would come to the house, would not know his family were elsewhere, so they'd be safer without him. All these matters were grinding through Arnold's mind, and try as he might, he just couldn't let go of any of them.

Kathy had been sleeping for a while, but suddenly she stirred. She reached out to Arnold with a gentle hand and murmured. "Can't sleep, honey?" She had sensed his restlessness, and she thought she understood why. "I'll get you some of the Xanax Frank gave me. It might get you a decent sleep for a few hours." She started to climb out of bed, but Arnold stopped her.

"It's okay, Kath," he said. "I'm going to go downstairs for a while; there's something I need to check."

He donned his dressing gown and slippers and quietly made his way down the stairs in the dark, not wanting to awaken anyone else. In his office he turned on a low light and his computer. He intended to spend some time checking the nature of the dreadful condition known as Lou Gherig's disease, more formally labeled Amytropic Lateral Sclerosis, or ALS. He found plenty of websites devoted to the subject, and in no time had confirmed what he'd already feared: Frank's long-term survival prospects were bleak. The early symptoms he was experiencing indicated another year or so of reasonable functionality followed by a miserable two years with severe breathing difficulties and pain, then a terminal decline of helplessness and total dependency, perhaps four years in total. Perhaps the most cruel fact of all, Arnold discovered, was that patients typically retained full mental functions throughout their ordeal, meaning that they knew just exactly what was happening to them and that they were doomed to suffer an awful physical imprisonment, becoming progressively more helpless with each passing day.

Arnold sat staring at the latest of the websites he had perused, just one of a dozen or more he had searched, hoping for a better picture from any one of them, but with no such luck. He sighed deeply and reached for his mouse, intent on logging off. In the still of this awful night, his mood made even worse by what he'd discovered on the Internet, he was suddenly startled by a shuffling sound behind him.

His office door creaked a little and Arnold turned to see who or what was intruding. The door opened wide and there, framed in the gloomy doorway, stood Frank, in his pajamas and a gown.

"What's up, Arnold?"

"You scared the hell out of me, Frank," Arnold said. "Did I disturb you?"

"No, I was awake. Heard you–or I assumed it was you–come down the stairs. I decided to join you, see what was up." He approached the computer and squinted at the screen.

Without glasses he couldn't be certain, but it sure looked like some sort of medical website.

"I might have known," he said, and he pulled a chair closer to where Arnold sat. "Satisfied by what you found?"

Arnold eyed his uncle for a few seconds, choosing not to respond.

"Okay, if that's the way you want to play it. Hey, you want something to eat, or drink? I'm kind of peckish."

"Yeah, me too. I thought maybe I'd warm some milk. Couldn't sleep. My mother used to warm milk for me, as a boy, when I couldn't sleep. Want some?"

Frank laughed a little. "She learned it from our mother, Arnold. They do that in England, you know. Cheaper than Scotch whiskey, I imagine. Sure sounds revolting, but I'll give it a try." Frank Dobson and his sister, Emily, Arnold's mother, both born in England, were brought to America as children shortly before World War II.

Arnold shut down his computer and the two men made their way to the kitchen. They allowed the light from the den to show their way, not wishing to turn on more lamps. The serving hatch through to the den also provided a little more light once they were in the kitchen; they had deliberately left on Arnold's desk lamp.

Arnold poured a measured pint of low-fat milk into a saucepan and placed it on the stove. Frank pulled two mugs from a cabinet and they both sat at the kitchen table, waiting, each uncertain what subject to tackle next.

Arnold broke the uneasy silence: "I want you and Hilda to sell your house and come live here, Frank, with us. We have plenty of room, and I'm certain there are good doctors in Portland who are up on–"

Frank reached out and placed a heavy hand on Arnold's, on the tabletop. He had a slight grin on his face.

"What?" Arnold said. "Don't give me a hard time, Frank. You could use the money you get from your house to–"

Frank's second interruption was verbal: "Why would you want to be burdened by a dying old man? For several years, likely."

Arnold placed his other hand on that of Frank and sighed. Slowly, he said, "I need to, Frank. I just need to be..." He then choked a little, his voice failing him.

Arnold had suffered with two prior losses; people he cared for taken by killer diseases. His mother, deserted by her drunken husband when Arnold was a mere boy, had died a painful and lingering death from Emphysema. Then, after many years of blissful marriage to his first wife, Mildred, Arnold had served as a loving caretaker as Mildred slowly died from breast cancer. The cruel disease finally won the protracted and brutal battle, but it had ravaged her body for many months. Arnold was devastated.

He finally found the words he'd tried for: "I would feel terrible, Frank, if I were not with you as you fight this thing. You mean far more to me than I can ever find a way to describe. So if you don't come here, I'll just have to come to be with you in

Pittsburgh." He then laughed, with considerable difficulty, trying hard for a little humor.

"God, did I just say I'd be willing to come live in Pittsburgh! I can't believe–"

An urgent interruption then came from the area of the stove. The milk boiled over with a loud sizzling noise as the bubbling froth hit the hot plate of the stovetop. Arnold reacted quickly, turning off the burner, but not before there was one hell of a mess, the spilled milk rapidly burning to a brown crust on the flat ceramic surface.

"Dammit!" he said angrily.

Frank came to his aid, but there was little they could do. The remaining milk was spoiled, having burned on the inside of the saucepan.

"Well, there went that idea," Arnold said, running cold water into the saucepan. "Want me to start again?"

Frank chuckled. "Hell, no. I don't even know why I agreed to hot milk in the first place. You got anything stronger? A glass of port will work a whole lot better than milk, especially burned milk."

Arnold, now giggling in concert with his uncle, found the port decanter and poured a few ounces into each of two sherry glasses. They sat down again and sipped the wine. Arnold sat eying the wine decanter oddly. "You know where I got this piece of crystal, Frank?"

"No idea. It's a nice one, I'll say that."

The wine decanter was a finely engraved one-liter lead crystal bottle that had an ornate etching of a sailing ship on it.

173

"My father brought this home one time. It must have been one of the few times he came home from a trip with anything of real value. Gave it to my mother, which was odd, because she didn't drink wine. It was the only thing I took from the house when she died. Other than a few pictures and a lot of bad memories, that is. I suspect old Jasper Towncraft stole this from someone."

Frank laughed, but he could tell that Arnold felt melancholy, and he knew exactly why. Arnold had been badly abused by his father, and for many years he had blamed his mother for not intervening, or for not taking her two children to safety, away from the drunken and mean philanderer her husband eventually became.

"Well, it's a fine keepsake, Arnold. Emily would be pleased you still have it. She loved you a great deal, you know. You and your sister."

Arnold said nothing for a while, still struggling with bitter memories of his impoverished childhood. Finally, he said, "I spoke with Victoria a few days ago. She asked if I'd heard from you lately."

"I should call her myself," Frank said. "She okay?"

"Yeah. Having hip problems, apparently. She's a great gal."

Arnold's sister, Victoria, who was older than Arnold by seven years, had run away from their abusive home in Pennsylvania when she was sixteen and had not been heard from for many years. Frank knew of her whereabouts all the time, and he actually helped her make a life for herself on the west coast. It was not until Arnold was nearing retirement that Victoria allowed

Frank to reveal her whereabouts. She lived a comfortable but simple life in a seaside community in Southern California, and so Arnold, after retiring, had made considerable effort to maintain a relationship with her, visiting her from time to time. More than forty years of total separation had not made the relationship as warm as perhaps it might have been otherwise, but there was a bond of sorts.

"Yes, she is," Frank said. "What about A-J? You spoken to him this summer?"

Arnold smiled. A-J was his grandson, a wonderful bonus he didn't even know a thing about until the boy was fifteen. Arnold had a teenage affair with an older woman named Dorothy, one of his teachers in high school. This brief but intense relationship had occurred in the summer, after Arnold had graduated, and when he went off to college the pregnant Dorothy decided to withhold the information of Arnold's baby, a daughter she named Dorothea. So Arnold never knew he had a child, and was destined to remain unaware of his grandson, Arnold Joseph, or A-J, for many years. Frank was the one who finally revealed A-J's existence to Arnold when the boy was fifteen years old, and Frank also made arrangements for the boy to meet his grandfather. That had been the beginning of a special relationship, and now A-J was attending Biddlington College, where Arnold had a lengthy and distinguished career as a professor of government.

"He's actually in Europe right now, Frank. Doing a summer course in Denmark, Copenhagen. He'll be back in a couple of weeks, and then he begins his senior year at Biddlington. Doing exceptionally well, I'm told."

Arnold had served on the Board of Regents at Biddlington College ever since his retirement, and he still had contacts there, Frank knew.

"What's he going to do after he graduates? Still no decision?"

"I hope he goes on to graduate school. He certainly has a mind for it; but I rather feel he has other plans. Doesn't say a whole lot about it to me. Or to his father."

"It must be tough for him at Biddlington; you were such a legend there."

"Hah. I think not. Any such legends that once existed have long ago dissolved, Frank. They never live long because they have no substance. The truth is that the most significant thing I ever did as a professor was prove that I didn't kill my two colleagues: the Dean and Patricia Slocum. And even in that endeavor you did the majority of the detective work."

Frank smiled, recalling the day he'd heard the disturbing news of Arnold's assumed guilt in two brutal on-campus murders. "Tell me the truth, now, Arnold," he said. "How long could you have tolerated those two lesbian leftists if that student hadn't bumped them off first?"

Arnold grinned, but he didn't answer. Frank knew his nephew was a pacifist, but he also knew just how frustrated he had become with the politically correct madness that had swept the Biddlington campus at the time. The student who killed two of Arnold's colleagues had skillfully framed Arnold, and for a time it looked as if he was going to be charged with the murders. But then Arnold recruited Frank, and the two of them not only proved Arnold's innocence, they also exposed the real killer. That had been their first case together.

"That was a challenging situation, wasn't it?" Frank said.

"Oh, yes. So was the case involving the crooked executives at Sontec Corporation. I especially enjoyed the final outcome of that one."

"Which reminds me, where is your neighbor? Jake, is it? Jake Farrow?"

"Aaah, the retired cop. They moved away a few months ago."

"Too bad. We sure put him to good use in that Sontec situation, didn't we?"

"Careful, Frank." Arnold chuckled. "We said we'd never talk about that again, and with good reason. Anyway, Jake was restless in retirement and he went back to work. He's now the chief of police in Reno. Say... I have a thought. The house next door is rented. Jake and his wife intend to move back here in five years, when his contract expires in Reno. You want me to see if his tenants there are long-term? If not, maybe you and Hilda could move in there."

"Five years, huh?" Frank's muttered response, and his tone, reflected his obvious thought: five years would be long enough for him.

"Don't even think that way, Frank," Arnold said, wagging a finger. "We're going to find a way to beat this thing." He went silent for a while, and then he said, "I'll talk to the folks next door. For the right kind of incentive they would surely be willing to move to another place. I could even buy a place and rent it to them, if they're at all flexible."

"I don't want you spending your money on me, Arnold."

"Nah. It would be a good investment. God knows I'm not getting great returns on my equities, and real estate is always good. Besides, this way you'd be close by without actually being in our hair, so to speak."

Frank grunted, noncommittal.

"Just think about it, Okay? You're not going to make me come live in a hell-hole like Pittsburgh, are you?"

Frank offered a curious smile. "No, I'll not wish that on you," he said. "Actually, Pittsburgh is not a bad place to live, even for a snobbish old professor, like you. And it would put you a lot closer to Biddlington College, right?"

"I only have to go to the college three or four times a year, Frank," Arnold said, ignoring the barb. He knew he was a snob. "I enjoy tossing in my two-cents worth into how the college should be run, at board meetings and such."

"I just bet you do," Frank said. "Do you have regular contacts with anyone at the college? Other than with the administration and the board, I mean."

"How did we get back to the subject of Biddlington again?" Arnold absently added a little more port to each glass. "Yeah, I do. Mostly with Middlecoff and a couple other friends on the faculty. As a matter of fact I had a call just a few days ago. Did you ever meet Bernie Dillon? He was in charge of admissions. God help us, he still is."

"No, never did meet him. I gather he's not one of your buddies. Was he asking you to do some recruiting?"

"I do some of that, at times, but his call was for personal reasons. He's written a book about higher education, he said. Wanted me to review the manuscript and perhaps write an introduction for it." Arnold suddenly started to chuckle. "Oh, my God. I just remembered something."

"What?"

"Well, Bernie was once on the faculty, but he never made tenure. No surprise there, but he was in a faculty meeting once, and he said there was no such thing as a book that had no value." Arnold was now laughing uncontrollably.

"What's so funny?" Frank asked, grinning but not really knowing why.

"Oh, this really is hilarious, Frank. Someone's response to Bernie's silly remark was, 'Maybe you'll write a book of your own some day, Bernie. And when you do you'll prove what you just said to be false'." Arnold had great difficulty getting these words out, laughing as hard as he was, but Frank fully understood what he was saying.

"Oh, that is cruel. So now he has a book. I bet he doesn't remember you were at that meeting."

"You got that right. Probably doesn't even remember that he said such an outrageous thing. But he is such a twit, Frank, it probably wouldn't matter if he did remember."

"Have you read the book?"

"Hell, no. I declined his kind offer. But I can guarantee that he has proved our colleague was right."

Now, both men were laughing, trying hard not to make too much noise. Each of them knew that the tension they felt was a factor in their silly reverie, but they also knew it was therapeutic.

There was a long pause. Finally, Arnold said, "I really do want you to think about moving here, Frank."

Frank remained noncommittal. "I'll think about it, " he said. "Right now we have more urgent business to attend to. Let's discuss your suggestion when we know Bryan Olmstead is safely behind bars again, okay? Let's drink to that goal."

"Yes. And also to a miraculous recovery for my dearest friend," Arnold said, his voice catching again, all humor now gone.

The two of them raised and clinked their glasses in the semi-darkness. Had there been a little more light, each of them would have seen the tears that glistened in the eyes of the other. They said little else for a while, each deep in thought. Then, as if rehearsed, they began to invent a series of feeble jokes about what Kathy would do to them for fouling up her immaculate stovetop. It was 2:55 A.M., so, after a few more minutes kibitzing, they made the rounds of the downstairs windows and doors, checking security for the second time that night, and they returned upstairs to their beds, each uncertain whether or not the wine would help them get a decent sleep. Each of them was filled with a myriad of emotions.

***

Bryan Olmstead was adept at breaking and entering. He had made a decent living at it over the last several years, entering

180

mostly private homes, and he was smart. He did it in daylight hours, while the homeowners were at work, the kids in school. He knew that in most middle-class families two people worked, these days, so he concentrated on homes that were ordinary but in upper-middle-class neighborhoods, where there was modest wealth but few complex security systems. He had made a number of important scores in several homes on his meandering journey from southern California north. He had even nabbed a fine Browning .22 caliber automatic pistol in one home, along with a box of ammunition. This gun had a rosewood handle, and he loved the heft of it, the way the polished grip fit his hand perfectly. He liked small caliber pistols. They did all the right things to a human brain when fired at close range, and yet they made a relatively quiet crack, especially when muffled by a pillow or a cushion. He had used this gun twice already, following brief and enjoyable encounters with unnamed young women in two California towns.

He still had his knife though, and he was ambivalent about which method of killing he preferred. He felt an especially powerful rush when he thrust the sharp blade of his knife into the gut of a woman. But killing them in any way was such a turn-on. Raping was deeply satisfying for his urge to brutalize, too, but the ultimate thrill was seeing the terror in their eyes when they realized their final moments of life were dwindling. Sometimes, when he used the knife, he would lick the blade afterwards. Tasting the hot salty fluid was like icing on the cake. As he contemplated these satisfactions, now, seated in his latest automobile, he drooled heavily, and he wiped it away from his chin with his shirtsleeve.

He eyed the impressive two-story home he had set as his next target, and he carefully estimated the options for entry. It was early afternoon, and there seemed to be no sign of life at the house. As luck would have it, Bryan had found this house standing all by itself on a large fenced lot located on a quiet country road. He could see other homes not far away, but far enough that his activities would not be spotted by a nosy neighbor. This break-in he'd not have any trouble with at all, he was sure. He drove on past the driveway a couple hundred yards and parked.

**Chapter Nineteen**

Frank had no luck trying to reach Art Segura the next morning. He first tried at 6:30 A.M., calling the detective's home after he'd enjoyed less than three hours of sleep, himself, and he tried again every ten minutes thereafter. He decided he'd try the detective's office soon after eight o'clock. Surely he would be on deck by then.

Arnold came downstairs at 7:15 and Brendan joined them within minutes. The two older men were with Brendan in Arnold's study when Segura finally called. He was in a rental car, he said, less than twenty miles away. Completely surprised, Frank asked what was going on.

"I am now quite sure that Bryan is somewhere near you, Frank. He must be, and I'll tell you why when I get there. Just give me directions to Arnold's house."

Frank did as he was asked, and then the three men continued their conversation while they waited for Segura to show up. Kathy had heard the commotion and the telephone ringing and she came downstairs, sleepy-looking, still in a dressing gown. She eyed her husband but decided not to ask the questions that burned in her mind. She offered to make breakfast,

183

and before she even had eggs in the skillet the two boys showed up, barefoot and in their pajamas. They offered to help Kathy and she cheerfully accepted, even though she knew their involvement would slow things down. And then detective Segura showed up, adding to Kathy's burden.

Frank reacted positively to Segura's statement that he had joined them to ensure their protection, and to recapture Olmstead when he showed up. He told Segura of their plan to take the women and children to the Riverside Motel, less than ten miles away, and the detective agreed that this was a smart move. He also took the time to go into detail as to why he had shown up unannounced, telling of the discovery that the murder in Madras had taken place in the home of an onion seed farmer.

"So it was him!" Brendan was obviously agitated. "I mean, I don't pick up psychic signals from anyone else... no one but Bryan, so I just knew. My God, that was two days ago, and Madras is less than eighty miles from here. He could be–"

"He has a cell phone," Segura said, interrupting deliberately. "It was stolen with a Buick automobile from a home in Barstow, probably the day after Bryan killed his mother. We are trying to track down calls that he may have made during the last two days from that phone. What we learn could tell us a whole lot about his recent movement."

"Where's Barstow?" Frank asked.

"It's half-way between LA and Vegas," Brendan said, but he gave the old ex-cop a quizzical look. "On I-10, the main interstate east out of southern California. Why?"

"Just trying to make sense of the sequence of events," Frank explained.

"Do you know for sure that Bryan really did kill his mother, Art?" Arnold asked. "And that he stole this Buick and the cell phone?"

"No, on both counts," Segura said. "But it seems highly probable. Who else that might have stolen the car would be killing people in the same way Bryan does, heading north all the time, in the direction of where you guys are located? We do know the Buick ended up in Central California, near Fresno. The Highway Patrol found it a couple of days ago, and–"

"Fingerprints, Art?" Frank asked.

"Your eggs are ready, gentlemen," Kathy said, sticking her head into Arnold's office through a small serving hatch she used when her husband was writing or reading quietly by himself. "If you all go into the dining room, I'll serve you there. That will leave the kitchen table for Rebecca, the boys and me. Honey, just put some place mats on the dining table, will you. I'll get Jason and Tommy to act as waiters."

Arnold regretted this last part of Kathy's offer; it meant that they would have to watch what they said while the two boys were around. No sense alarming them. But he complied with her request anyway and the four men relocated, seated themselves at the dining table, where they continued talking.

"How long will you be here?" Frank asked Segura. "And how did you manage to get away? I mean how did you get approval to be out of jurisdiction like this?"

Art grinned. "I didn't. Even when the lieutenant was told about the onion farm he still said no. So I just took it upon myself. I may not have a job when I get back home. But at least that means, in answer to your first question, I can stay here as long as it takes. Now that Olmstead seems certainly headed this way, across state lines, I should get the FBI involved. I hate when the Feds get into the act. By the way, I spoke with Tim Bartholome yesterday. Persuaded him to head back south, to go on home. No sense him bringing his family to where they would be–"

The two boys came in then, each carrying two plates of ham and eggs, both with knives and forks in rolled cloth napkins tucked under each arm–quite a feat for such youngsters. Jason almost allowed the eggs to slide off one of his plates, but he reacted in time. Kathy followed them with a tray of coffee and mugs, also four large glasses of orange juice. "Anything else I can get you boys?" she asked cheerily as she poured coffee.

Segura apologetically asked for ketchup, and Frank said he'd like pepper and salt, so the two boys rushed off to oblige. Kathy took advantage of the boys' brief absence, asking, "Okay, Detective Segura, tell me you're here on a social visit, and see if I believe that. Something bad is about to happen, isn't it?"

"We don't know that, sweetheart," Arnold said. "Art is here as a precaution, that's all, and you don't need to–"

"You really expect me to buy that, Arnold?" Kathy smiled sarcastically, her eyes open wide in a glare of defiance, and this silenced her husband. The others seemed unwilling to say anything, either, and they all quietly began to eat their breakfast.

The boys brought the condiments and returned to the kitchen, where they continued to hinder Kathleen, chatting endlessly.

"You were able to reach Tim?" Brendan asked the cop after a while. "I haven't spoken with him for two days."

"He called me," Segura said. "He was actually glad to head for home, and since we're now pretty sure that he was never under threat, we–"

"But he was being followed, Art; by some guy in a Buick!"

"I don't think he ever was, Brendan. And, as a matter of fact, we think Bryan Olmstead never caught the significance of the message left on the Arcata girl's message machine by Tim's daughter. Either that or he chose to ignore the Bartholome family completely. So Tim and his family were never in Bryan's crosshairs. That's what I now think."

"You think? That's not particularly reassuring. What about the killing in June Lake? You saying that was not Bryan either?"

Segura sighed deeply. "Probably not. We'll know for sure maybe today, but Bryan doesn't decapitate his victims." He looked at the others closely, one by one, and calmly said, "Bryan Olmstead is somewhere near here, I'm certain of it. In fact I have staked my career on it. No sense asking Tim to come join us, placing himself and his family in jeopardy."

"You didn't answer my earlier question, Art," Frank said, "about fingerprints and such, in or on the Buick."

"Nothing useable. But we did find a small carpet fiber in the Buick that matches what's on the floor in Sarah Olmstead's

187

home. But it's a cheap carpet, sold by many do-it-yourself stores, so this is not conclusive."

"What about DNA evidence from the victim in June Lake?"

"As I said, another day; two at the most. Listen, I think you're doing the right thing to get the women and children away from here," Segura said soberly. He looked at his watch briefly and added, "In fact, you'd better hustle and get on with that program. Since I am now here, Brendan, you'd better plan on staying at the hotel with your family and Kathleen, to provide some protection for them. You have a gun?"

"Me? Hell, no."

"I have a spare handgun in my bag, so take it with you. Frank, you have a piece?"

Frank nodded solemnly, seeming distracted, deep in thought. "What about progress on the phone trace, Art. How soon will you have results?"

"It will take a while. I called it into our people and they'll get the service provider on it right away. But I'm not optimistic on that front. It's a cell phone number, like I said, and Bryan's likely on the move. They'll soon be able to tell us where he was at the time phone calls are made... but unless he remains in the same location, or makes many calls, we'll be out of luck. Like I said, if he's on the move... well, you get the picture."

"At least we'll know if he's headed in this direction, right?" Arnold asked.

"I think we already know that," Segura said quietly. He had a grave expression on his face. "My guess is that he's somewhere close to Brendan's house right now. There's really no way he can know Brendan and his family are here, so I asked the Marion County sheriff to send a squad car over there this morning, just to be sure he isn't there already."

Brendan's eyes flashed, showing a new level of alarm at what he'd heard. Again he was wondering if Bryan had the ability to detect his location by psychic means, ESP, or whatever, but he said nothing to the others about this, and he continued eating. As they all did, rushing to finish.

They started to pile up their plates, intent upon taking them to the kitchen, but they were interrupted by the telephone. Arnold quickly stepped to his office to take the call, but it was for Segura. He called the detective in, saying, "It's a Lieutenant Jones for you, Art."

Segura sighed, muttering something incomprehensible as he took the phone from Arnold's hand.

Brendan had gone upstairs to hurry Rebecca through her dressing and packing process, and also to pack his own immediate needs. He knew he could always come back to the Towncraft house for essentials, as needed, but he also knew there would be risks in doing so. It would be difficult, keeping the children cooped up inside their motel room all day, but for a while they could manage He hoped it would not be longer than three or four days. Nevertheless, he urged Rebecca to take as much of her clothing as she could squeeze into one suitcase with his own few things. The tension in his voice apparently affected Rebecca; suddenly she stopped what she was doing and started to sob. Brendan rushed to her side and hugged her close.

"I know what you're feeling, sweetheart," he said softly. "But it'll all be over soon."

Rebecca swallowed hard and cleared her throat. "Don't you think we'd be safer if we all stayed here?" she said. "Now that Detective Segura is here, surely we–"

"I'm going to be with you," Brendan said calmly. "Segura suggested it, and I agreed to take a gun with me, so–"

"A gun? Oh, no. I hate guns, you know that."

"So do I, sweetie, but I'll be able to protect you if Bryan finds out where we are. Come on, I think we have enough things in this bag. Let's go pack for the boys."

Brendan knew he had to keep Rebecca busy. It would help prevent her from thinking too much about the terror that could rapidly descend upon them at any moment.

Downstairs, Segura had finished talking to his boss and had several new things to report. He called Frank and Arnold back into the office and closed the door.

"Olmstead was involved in two more murders in Northern California," he said gravely. "One not far south of the Bay Area, probably two days ago. And another, a day later, in a place called Redding, two hundred miles from the Bay Area on the main interstate north."

Arnold sat down slowly and eyed the detective. "Exactly when was the killing in Madras, Art?"

"I know what you're thinking, Arnold. And this certainly raises a question or two. We think the girl in Madras was killed three days ago, just two days after the one in June Lake. And Madras is many miles north of these latest two, so you're thinking it would make no sense for him to go back south, after Madras. But let me remind you this guy is a maniac, no telling what he's up to. He has appetites that... Well, you know what he's like. The truth is we—"

"How do you know the Bay Area killing and the one in Redding are Bryan's handiwork, Art?" Frank asked. "You have direct evidence?"

"Fingerprints." Segura showed no sign of resentment about Frank's probing; in fact he seemed to welcome it. "He got careless this time," he said. He left all kinds of prints in the public library in Redding and partials in both these victims' automobiles. These two were shot, execution style, back of the head, small caliber handgun. Ballistics show that the gun was stolen from a private home in the Fresno area, four days ago."

Frank was now up and pacing, his limp showing, but he seemed not to be aware of his own discomfort. "Let me see if I have this straight, Art," he said. "Fresno is, what, two-hundred miles or more south of San Francisco?" He grabbed a map of California from Arnold's bureau and opened it quickly, donning his reading glasses. "Here it is. So this is where the Buick was found, what, four days ago?" he pointed at the town's location on the map.

"Actually, it was in a place called Tulare, not far from Fresno, but the car could have been there for a few days. We have no way of knowing, exactly."

"Okay, but a day later a Fresno house is burglarized and a hand gun stolen. Now, that same handgun may be in the hands of

Bryan Olmstead, and he has killed two young women with it. Both victims were raped, right?"

"Yes, brutally. Tied up with duct tape, raped and dumped with no clothes on their ravaged bodies. This is exactly the same pattern as before he was arrested the first time, and–"

"But don't you see the problem, Art? If he came up as far as Madras, here in Oregon," again he pointed, "and killed there to satisfy his vile urges, and assuming he came up here to deal with Brendan, Arnold and me, why the hell would he go all the way back down to the Bay Area, or even just as far as Redding?"

"Like I said; this man is a maniac. We aren't sure he knows where you all are, Frank. Maybe he came up to Madras just wandering, seeking prey. I had a case once, where–"

"All of that could well be true, Art, but on the other hand, Bryan may well have found out, from the Arcatas, where his brother's house is located. But even so, the Arcatas would know nothing about me and Arnold."

"That makes my argument even more valid, Frank. Olmstead may just be wandering aimlessly, has only a vague notion of getting his brother. Or he intends to do that but is enjoying his primary game along the way."

"So why are you here, instead of camped out on Brendan's doorstep?"

Segura could see the point of Frank's question clearly, and he had no answer other than that he was here to protect them all. "I am here simply because you're all here," he said. But then, as if by some synchronistic magic, the phone rang, and this call made Frank's questions irrelevant. Arnold answered the phone in his usual manner: "Towncrafts."

There was silence for a second, and then a male voice said, quietly and slowly, "Tell Brendan I'm on my way. And after him, you're next, professor."

Arnold's face went deathly white. He heard the line go dead and returned the handset to its charging cradle. Turning to the others, he said, "That was Bryan Olmstead. My God, Frank, he does know us, and he knows where we are. Or me, at any rate."

Segura checked the caller ID window on Arnold's phone and compared what he saw with the number of the cell phone presumed to be stolen with the Barstow Buick. "You're right, Arnold," he said. "That was him. Did he identify himself?"

Arnold sat down slowly and glared at Segura. "How did he find me?"

"What did he say, Arnold," Segura said urgently. "Tell me his exact words."

"He must be in Brendan's house," Towncraft said. "How else would he know about me? Art, for god's sake, he has already been in Brendan's house!"

"Let's not be so hasty, Arnold. Just exactly what did Bryan say to you on the phone?"

Arnold thought for second or two before replying: "Tell Brendan I'm on my way. And after him, you're next, professor."

"That's it? Nothing more?"

"No, just those few words."

"When you answered the phone, you used your name, right?"

Arnold hesitated again, seeming uncertain. "I'm not sure I did. I would usually say my name, but I... I'm not sure."

Frank said, "Yes, you sure did, Arnold." He then moved to the telephone and pushed the button that played back Arnold's outgoing message: "Towncraft residence. Leave a name and number, we'll get back to you."

"He may have called here at some other time, guys," Frank said. "You ever get a message indicator, Arnold, and when you play it back there's no message?"

"Yes, we do. Not often, but occasionally. An unlisted number is not immune to peddlers, you know. In fact there was one such just yesterday afternoon. But even if Bryan made a call here at some prior time, and verified who and where I am in that way, he would still have had to obtain this number from someone in the first place."

Frank could see Arnold's point. "I wonder if Brendan told anyone where he was going to be for these few days?" he said. "At his office, maybe?"

"Call Brendan's home right now," Segura said. "See what message he has on his answering machine."

Arnold pushed his speed-dial number seven, and nervously he waited. *What if Brendan was there, and he answered this call?* Soon, after just two rings, he heard the voice of Jason Carlson say, "Carlson residence. We're not home, so leave a message. If you're calling for Brendan, he can be reached at his office, two-two-six, six-six-three-one."

194

The three men exchanged puzzled glances, each laden with various concerns.

"I'd better call the cell phone company," Segura said. "They have been monitoring that mobile phone since last night. With luck they will know where this call originated."

While the detective was making his call, Arnold turned to Frank and said in a voice noticeably altered by tension, "He somehow knows that Brendan brought his family here, Frank. My God, it's less than two hours from Brendan's place to here. If he left there this morning, he could be right outside, watching as Brendan takes his family off to the motel. He will follow them. We can't let that happen."

"We'll get to that problem in a minute," Segura said, having hung up. He had overheard Arnold's anxious statement. "Where did Brendan go?"

"He's upstairs. Want me to go get him?" It was Jason, standing just inside the doorway of Arnold's office, looking frightened. As focused as the three adults had been, they had not seen the youngster come into the office. Now, they each wondered how long he had been standing there, and what he had learned.

"Yeah, go ahead and get him, son," Frank said.

"That's unfortunate," Arnold said when he heard the boy's footsteps on the stairs. "But it can't be helped, now. What did you find out, Art? On the phone?"

"I suspect those two boys know more than we think they do, but it can't be helped. As for the phone call, I gave them this number and they'll call back soon, I expect. Look, let's not be too hasty. There's nothing new here, really, just because Bryan called. The son-of-a-bitch is brazen as hell, but we already knew that. We also knew he was headed this way, so–"

"But the fact that Bryan called here means that he–"

"Bryan called here?" Brendan burst into the room, his voice registering alarm. "What did he say? Where the hell is he?"

"Take it easy, Brendan," Art said. "No call for alarm. Listen, did you tell anyone you were coming here? Someone at the office, maybe?"

"Oh, shit!" Brendan said, sitting down on one of the small armchairs. "I never dreamed... I was expecting a couple of calls from key accounts, so I gave my secretary this number. Bryan must have... I'm sorry, Arnold. I never dreamed–"

"Don't worry about it, Brendan," Arnold said, now seeming somewhat more relaxed by the fact that they had a possible explanation. "At least we now know he definitely plans to come here. And we are ready for him, right? Everybody?"

Again the phone rang, and this time Segura took the call himself. After a brief exchange on the line, he hung up and said, calmly, "The Madras killing was not Olmstead, people. The DNA did not match. Same thing with the one in June Lake."

There was a stunned silence.

"But how can that be, Art?" Brendan looked shocked. "The onions! I smelled the onions, and you said it was done at an onion farm. I don't get it."

"I cannot explain that, Brendan. I really can't. But DNA doesn't lie. What they found of the killer's DNA in Madras is a complete mismatch for Bryan Olmstead."

"Could there be some sort of mistake at the lab? Is that possible? My visions were very clear, and there was definitely an onion smell. A very strong onion smell."

"Lab mistakes can happen, sure, but the labs we use have carefully controlled procedures. Anyway, you admit that you don't see all of Bryan's killings, right? You haven't seen these latest two, so maybe the mistakes are yours?" Segura knew this would upset Brendan, but he could see that Brendan had become fixated on this apparent flaw in his dream perceptions. Anyway, there was important work to do, and no time to waste.

"Don't worry about it Brendan. Just get the women and the children off to the Riverside Motel. Make sure you all stay inside until we have good news to report. As you leave here, keep a sharp eye out for anyone following you. Get settled in quickly, lock your doors and windows. You need anything, call here, okay?"

Rebecca and Kathleen were ready, so they all gave everyone a hug and piled into Brendan's Cadillac, with Kathleen and the two boys in the back seat. The boys waved frantically as their father drove off, apparently treating the whole thing as an adventure. But despite outward appearances, Jason, the oldest by more than two years, had heard enough of the conversation among the three men in Arnold's study that he had many unanswered questions. He went quiet on the road, planning how and when he would ask his father to explain their moves. He knew something was amiss, but he didn't exactly know what.

When Arnold and Frank returned to the house, having left Segura inside to pick up the phone, Arnold said to the detective,

"Listen, Art, Brendan is not the only one puzzled about the onion farm question. I'm equally baffled. He may well have not always had psychic visions of every killing by Bryan, as you said, but for every one that he has experienced, he has always been right on."

"I don't know what to tell you, Arnold," Art said. "We're in an area that no detective has ever been comfortable with. Right, Frank?"

"Psychic phenomena?" Frank grinned. "Oh yeah." He was having some difficulties with his one leg. Arnold had seen him rubbing it and turning his ankle vigorously from side to side in an apparent attempt to ease the discomfort or maybe to stop the twitching. "That's certainly true, Art. But there's surely more than one onion farm in the world, don't you think?"

"It would be one hell of a coincidence if there were two killings on an onion farm in the same week, Frank. And we've checked all the 1-87's up and down the west coast."

Frank thought for a second or two, and then he said, "What if no body was found? For the one Brendan visualized, I mean. There are only 1-87 bulletins once the cops get involved, right? Once there is a confirmed killing."

Art knew the wily old ex-cop was right, but he said, "Then Bryan needs to get busy and identify the place where his brother's victim is hidden. I can't do anything about a body that hasn't been found."

The oppressive tension had produced a level of friction between these three, and it was now starting to show..

## Chapter Twenty

But the next piece of news that came to the Towncraft house eased their tensions quite a bit. Brendan and the others had not been gone more than twenty minutes when Segura received another call. This one informed him that the cell phone call from Bryan had been made from the town of Redding. He was evidently still in California.

"How the...?" Arnold was plainly baffled. But with help from Frank and Segura, he soon came to realize that Bryan Olmstead had never made it as far as Brendan's home. Instead, he had picked up Brendan's work number and called it. They would have passed on Towncraft's phone number, assuming the query was from a customer, just as Brendan had asked them to do

Arnold called Brendan with the good news about his brother's current whereabouts, but despite this encouraging revelation, Brendan was obviously still deeply concerned about the failure of his vision.

"Well, that makes my decision so much easier, Arnold," Brendan said. "I have the time, now, so I'm going to drive over to Madras, or to Warm Springs, and find the Serbein farm for myself. I'd like to find out what that house looks like. I must do this. I hope you understand."

"Brendan, I don't think that's a good–" The phone went dead before Arnold could say more. He turned to the others and told them what Brendan had said.

"That's a God-damned fool-of-a-thing to do," Segura said. "Call him right back, let me talk to him."

"No, wait," Frank said. "Let him go, Art. I fully understand why he wants to do this, and we know where Bryan is, right? It's not much more than an hour's drive to Madras, so he'll be back before dark. Bryan is hours away from here; so let him satisfy his curiosity, or whatever is plaguing him. No harm done. I'll go over to the motel to be with the women and children until he gets back."

Segura nodded in agreement, but he was plainly uneasy. Arnold was also disturbed by his young friend's impetuous decision, but he could see Frank's point.

"All right, Frank," Arnold said. "Have a cup of coffee before you go, why don't you. It seems we really do have a little time, now. Say, have you called Hilda, lately? This might be a good time. Give her Kath's number at the motel would you. If they can chinwag for a while it will help Kathleen relax a bit. Their number's written down on this scratchpad. Art and I will leave you in here, for privacy."

Arnold and Segura went to the kitchen, where Arnold made hot chocolate. The two of them sat down at the kitchen table and began a conversation that Segura found curious.

"How long have you been a cop, Art?" Arnold asked.

Segura grunted, and he raised an eyebrow in a comical way. "Seems like a million years," he said. "Actually, it's only thirty-three, but... I went to the academy right after serving in 'Nam. I was a marine for five years, right out of high school."

"So you're in your fifties now. That right?"

"Fifty-four." Segura said with a sigh. "Going on sixty-three."

"If you retired now, would you get a decent pension?"

"I'd get– You know, these are very strange questions, Professor. Why are you asking them, here, now?"

"He's just a nosy bugger, Art." Frank had evidently not been able to connect with his wife, and he entered the kitchen in time to hear Segura's query. "Actually, I think he's a little jealous of cops. Right, Arnold?" Frank poured coffee for himself and joined them at the table. "Are there any of Kathy's good cookies left?"

"Are you kidding?" Arnold said, "With two young boys in the house?"

Frank laughed. "Like bionic vacuum cleaners, aren't they? So why were you asking Art about his pension?"

"It'll soon be lunchtime, Frank. You shouldn't be snacking on anything. I was just getting ready to offer Art a job. You got a problem with that?"

The detective and Frank exchanged puzzled glances, neither having a clue what Arnold was talking about. Segura put down his mug and said, "I might well need a job, in fact. I was only half kidding when I said what I did at breakfast. The truth is—with what I said to my boss and then coming up here without approval—I may really be out of work when I get back home."

"That's what got me thinking, Art," Arnold said. "What you said earlier, I mean. You have no family, as I recall. So what's your current income?"

"I told you he was a nosy bugger," Frank said, grinning.

"You serious, Arnold?" Segura said. "What kind of job are we talking about?"

"Frank and I are in the crime detection business, we—"

"We are?" Frank said. "That's news to me. What he means, Art, is that Arnold thinks *he's* in the private eye business, but he's not. It's true that we've solved, or helped solve, a couple of crimes—"

"Shut up for a minute, you old fart," Arnold growled. "Just listen to what I have to say. I want the three of us to form a company that helps solve crimes. Preferably corporate crimes, like the one we worked on in the case of Sontec Corporation, or maybe government related fraud and such, but—"

"Arnold is on the board of directors for Sontec, Art. We found out that their senior management were screwing shareholders, and we actually solved a rather serious caper that involved millions of dollars. But he's—"

Arnold interrupted again: "Don't forget the murders, Frank. That son-of-a-gun was killing people who got in his way."

"Okay, you're right. But I honestly think those kinds of crime should be left to the authorities. The FBI has huge teams devoted to corporate crime. We have no special talent for it, and we could never get the resources it would take to do a creditable job. Besides, my working days are over."

"That's why we need a younger man involved, Frank. That's why we need somebody like Detective Segura, here."

Segura had been quiet up to this point, but now he said, "My salary is now seventy-three grand, Arnold, give or take a few bucks. If I retired right now, I'd get roughly forty-five a year for the rest of my life." There was an inquisitive gleam in his eye; he liked what he'd heard, so far. He stared hard at the professor, attempting to measure his level of commitment to what he was suggesting.

"Would you lose any of your pension if you went on somebody else's payroll?"

"No. Most cops who retire in their fifties take other jobs. I had always assumed I would do that too. But I'm not sure I'd be any good as a private eye. Tell me more about your plans though."

"Well, I was going to make this suggestion to Frank, but he's right about one thing: He's too damned old for the heavy road work we'd need from our main operative investigator, so he'll be our internal consultant and advisor." Arnold eyed his uncle, hoping he had not taken offense at this jab. He was certainly hesitant to say anything about Frank's illness, which he knew would soon become debilitating.

"Here's the thing, guys," Arnold went on, "more and more there are various so-called "white-collar" crimes being committed, often by senior people in large corporations. All too often these firms want no publicity, and they sure as hell don't want the Feds snooping around. We would offer our services to uncover such suspected crimes, do all the investigative work to reveal the facts when shareholders or executives become suspicious. The same thing goes for governmental fraud at all levels. That congressman in California, whatever his name is, was just the tip of the iceberg, I fear, The FBI will not act on suspicion alone, and ever since 9/11 they have been focusing much of their resources on terrorist threats. I have enough connections in big business, and also in government circles, so I can–"

"Arnold is on two corporate boards, Art. He has also served two presidents as an advisor… when he was an academic egghead. These days, he is merely a retired egghead. An old fart retired egghead who thinks he can do detective work."

Arnold smiled, ignoring Frank's comment, but then he surprised both his guests. "Look, there's big money to be made at this game," he said, now agitated. "I'm dead serious, guys. I will put up the money to form the company and pay all operating expenses until we get positive cash flow. Each of you will get a starting salary of eighty thousand a year and all expenses, plus twenty-five percent of any profits we make. And we'll do very well, once we get rolling. There would be no need for us to open an office, for now. We could do it all out of this house. Frank is moving in next door, and Art, you can also–"

"I'm doing what?" Frank asked.

Arnold seemed surprised. "Like I told you, Frank, you and Hilda can move into the house next door. I'll talk to–"

"You have no way of knowing if you can persuade the folks next door to move out, like you suggested. They could tell you to go to hell, Arnold. You know that."

"Everybody has a price, Frank. I'm sure I can get that done. But if not, there are other homes in the area. We'll need a place for Art too. You'd have no difficulty moving up here, would you Art?"

Segura was flabbergasted. "So I could take my pension and work for... work with you two and draw a salary of eighty grand? Is that what you're saying?"

"Plus a share of the profits, Art. And a car, plus a living allowance, of course."

Segura's face revealed his state of mind at that moment. He realized that the dreams he had recently been having, his hopes for a more peaceful life away from the dramatic slayings he always dealt with were... well, it all seemed so perfect. Maybe too perfect? "I hate to bring this up, gentlemen," he said, his hands spread before him as if to restore sanity to the conversation and to his two companions, "but we have a problem or two that needs to be dealt with before we begin any grand schemes to save the corporate world and our government from embezzlers and such. We have Bryan Olmstead to deal with."

Arnold nodded his head in agreement. "You're right, Art, of course. But hold these thoughts, we'll get back to them real soon." He looked at the kitchen wall clock and was amazed at how much time had passed since breakfast. "What time was it when Olmstead called here?" he asked.

Segura consulted his small notebook. "Five before ten. And he was in Redding at the time. I know what you're thinking, Arnold. And the answer is that he could be in this area by about four-o'clock this afternoon if he comes straight here. We should make plans for greeting him."

"I didn't ask how Hilda's doing, Frank," Arnold said. "Everything all right?"

"She was out on the beach, walking Shannon, her folks' dog. The temperature is in the high seventies, her mother said. Clear skies, just perfect. She's in Cape Cod, Art. With her folks."

"I've never been to Cape Cod," Segura said. "I was stationed at Camp Lejeune for a while, thirty-odd years ago. That's the closest I ever got to New England."

"Where were you born, Art?" Frank asked.

"East LA. My father was a Mexican, my mother Irish. Two good Catholics should have had more children, but it didn't work out that way, so I was an only child. They split up when I was in Nam. When I mustered out I got married, but that didn't last even four years. No kids, been on my own ever since." Segura seemed sad all of a sudden, and Frank decided to change the subject. He could relate well to Art Segura's family situation:

"I have no children either, sad to say. Or maybe it's a good thing? But at least my wife stuck by me when I was a cop. If I'd stayed on the force for many years, however, who knows what would have happened."

"The stats on that are pretty dismal, Frank," Segura said flatly. "As I'm sure you know."

Frank grunted his reply. "What say we grab an early lunch?" he said. "That will give us ample time to get ready for our unwelcome guest."

## Chapter Twenty-One

Brendan had also decided on an early lunch. It was not that he was hungry, but he felt sure he'd seen someone following him, in his rear-view mirror. He had Jason in the car with him, and now he had some reservations about that decision. He'd managed to persuade Rebecca to let the boy go along by telling her that Bryan was still far to the south of them, and certainly he knew that must be the case. He also felt reasonably assured that he and Jason would be back with them all, at the motel, long before they might be threatened by Bryan's arrival. Anyway, Bryan would know nothing about their hiding place. But, despite these realities, and the fact that Bryan couldn't possibly know where he was, Brendan still felt remarkably ill-at-ease. It was as if Bryan were nearby, and yet he knew that was not possible.

He had first spotted the car behind him when they were passing through the small town of Durfur, and he'd kept an eye on it all the way. There were other cars, but this one was always there, maybe half a mile back. It was hard to tell the make, but it was white, probably a Japanese import. He was approaching Madras, where he felt sure there would be a selection of restaurants, but up ahead he saw a sign for a place called *The Cooked Goose,* and he slowed the car.

"Why are we stopping, Dad?" Jason asked. The boy had been quiet, listening to his miniature I-pod music system—a birthday gift his parents had told him was a one-time thing, it being so expensive.

"I thought we'd eat early," Brendan said. "That okay with you?"

"This place looks pretty fancy," Jason said. "I'm not very hungry, Dad."

Brendan watched as the white car flashed by them, a Toyota, maybe five years old. He could see very little of the driver's face, however, as he seemed to be blowing his nose on a tissue. *Did that mean the man was trying to hide his face? Nah. Forget it! Bryan is a long way from here, and you know it!*

They went inside the restaurant and found that it was not really fancy after all. It had an unusual menu, however, with many vegetarian and low-fat offerings. Brendan opted for a bowl of cucumber soup and Jason asked for a grilled cheese sandwich, even though it was not on the menu. The waitress obliged, anyway, and she brought them both a drink of diet soda. "Soda-Pop," Jason said as they were served the drinks.

"What?" Brendan said.

"Uncle Arnold calls this stuff soda-pop."

Brendan laughed, though he was still feeling uneasy. He kept watch through the window as they ate their lunch, but he saw no white Toyota enter the restaurant parking lot. He decided to quit being paranoid.

When they returned to their car, Brendan pushed the steering wheel button that activated his On-Star phone. He instructed the system, with the mechanical voice that sounded female, to dial the numbers for the Riverside Motel. Once connected, he asked for the room number and Rebecca answered. "I just knew it would be you," she said. "Where are you?"

"About five miles north of Madras. We just ate lunch, should be in Warm Springs within twenty minutes. Everything okay there?"

"No problems. Frank calls us every few minutes. He's coming over here later. Such a love, he is. What did Jason have for lunch?"

"Guess."

"Don't tell me a grilled cheese sandwich?"

"What else?"

"I miss you two already, Bren. What time will you be home?"

"I miss you too, babe. I'd guess about three-thirty, maybe four."

"Okay, drive carefully, sweetheart."

Brendan's emotions were mixed and extremely complicated. He really wanted to be with his wife and his two boys. Instead, he was on a mission that made little sense now; he knew that all too well. He wondered if he would have been foolish enough to take this trip if he'd not learned that Bryan was still far away. He hoped not, but then again, this did feel rather like a compulsion. He just had to know for sure that what he'd seen in his vision was not the site of the Serbein Farm, and the slaughter of a young woman there, a girl named Suzie Carrow.

"You okay, Dad?" Jason asked after a few more minutes driving.

"Yeah, I'm fine. Why?"

"I dunno. You seem far away, sort of. You're worried about something bad, aren't you?"

Brendan reached out and tousled his son's hair. He grinned at him and said, "Yeah, something's bothering me. But it'll be just fine, don't you worry."

Jason picked up his music system again and placed the bud-like earphones in each ear. He seemed temporarily satisfied by what he'd heard from his father.

Soon they were in Madras, and Brendan found State Highway 26, turned north, his anxiety mounting rapidly as they closed in on his destination. They were now less than twenty miles from the place he was convinced had been his brother's killing site, just days before. *But maybe not?* In a few miles they crossed over and then ran alongside the Deschutes river, and Brendan slowed down a little, watching a couple of fly fishermen in float boats, trying for the famous Deschutes trout. He made a mental note that he should come back this way with Rebecca and the boys. He should work a little less, he knew; take vacation time, relax and enjoy life. These vague promises, he realized, were the result of the bizarre things that were happening, but he also knew they made sense.

They drove into Warm Springs slowly, and on the main street they stopped at the Post Office, where Brendan consulted the local phone book. He soon found the name Serbein, Henry, but the address, as he had suspected, was a Rural Route. He had no idea how to find the farm on that information, so he decided to consult the solitary clerk behind the counter. Perhaps she would know?

"Oh, yeah," she said cheerfully. "You with that magazine? Your colleague was here yesterday."

"No, I'm not a journalist," Brendan said quickly. "What magazine?"

"I forget the name. Some fancy magazine from Seattle. The name didn't mean anything to me. So why do you want to go out to the Serbein's place? You have a valid reason? They don't really need people just dropping by, you know. They have a right to privacy."

Brendan remembered the fact that the Serbeins grew onions, so he decided to lie, rather than appear foolish: "I'm with the State Department of agriculture, Debby," he said. The clerk wore a brass nametag. "I have business with Henry."

"Okay," she said, looking partly satisfied. "Well, if you drive north on 26 you'll come to a county road that goes off to the east, just two miles from the traffic lights. Another two miles along that road you'll see the Serbein farm, on the right. You'll likely smell the onions before you get there; there's no mistaking it at this time of year. The wind's in the right direction today, or you'd be able to follow your nose." She grinned.

Brendan thanked the woman and left, taking Jason by the hand. Jason still had both earphones plugged in, so he hoped the boy had not heard him lie. He and Becky had tried very hard to teach the boys about honesty, and the need for honorable behavior at all times. When they were back in the car, however, Jason removed one earphone and asked, "How come you told that lady you work for the Department of Agriculture, Dad?"

Brendan sighed. He decided he'd better tell the boy part of the story why they were here, in this small town. He excluded the gory details, and he neglected to say that Bryan Olmstead was his twin brother, but he simply said that a man by that name had killed a girl here, at a farmhouse. "For some reason, Jase, and I guess I'll never fully understand how, I sort of saw that killing take place, in my mind. I came here because I just have to be sure of what I saw."

Jason thought for a few seconds, and then he said, "You mean you had a dream or something?"

"Something like that, yeah."

"I had a dream not long ago that I hit a home run in a big game. I told you about it, remember? But it never came true."

"Well, maybe it will, Kiddo. One of these days."

"Daaad! Nobody my age ever hits a homer. I'm just a kid."

Brendan laughed. "You're not just any kid, Jason Carlson. You're one of the two best kids on this old planet." He was hoping Jason had forgotten his lie, but evidently he had not.

"So you lied to the Post Office lady because you didn't want her to know about your dream?"

"Yeah, I guess so. People wouldn't believe it, right? Most people wouldn't, I'd guess."

Jason went quiet, returning the earphone to his ear, and Brendan felt relieved that the boy had put the matter aside. They drove on in silence for a bit, going past a gas station that was in front of a small market. There, he spotted a white Toyota Celica, standing by the gas pumps. No one was in or near the car, so Brendan assumed the driver must be inside the store. He was tempted to stop, check it out, but he knew he would feel foolish, so he drove on. And then he spotted the farm. He slowed down and turned into the narrow dirt road that led to the farmhouse and outbuildings. He lowered the window on his side and instantly recognized the smell: rotting onions.

As Brendan approached the house, now driving very slowly, he saw a dog emerge from behind the barn and it came trotting toward them amiably. It looked like an Australian Sheepdog. Jason saw him too, and asked, "What kind of dog is that, Dad? Such a pretty color."

The dog stood wagging his tail as Jason opened his car door, and he fussed a great deal at the head pat he received from this stranger that had come visiting his master.

"He's an Australian Sheepdog, Jason," Brendan said. "Come and pat him, he's real friendly."

"That he is, but I wish he weren't so damned friendly sometimes." A man had emerged from the house, stood on the front porch glaring at Brendan and the boy. "Come, Frosty," he ordered the dog. Frosty obeyed immediately, running to his master's side, where he sat and joined the staring game.

"That is one fine dog, sir," Brendan said. "You must be Mr. Serbein."

"And who might you be? I hope you're not another of them television people."

Brendan stepped a little closer, trying hard to figure out what to say. He had rehearsed many opening lines, but they all seemed silly now that he was here. "I'm really sorry to disturb you, sir, because I know that what happened here a few days ago must have been a dreadful thing. But I think I might be the brother of the man who did this. I'm here to make sure of that, and to offer my–"

"Get off my property!" Serbein ordered coldly. "We've had enough visitors in the last two days to last us a lifetime. So just turn that fancy car around and get back on the road."

Brendan was about to do as he had been ordered, but Jason spoke up. "Dad, Detective Segura said this killing wasn't done by Bryan Olmstead. You heard him, I know you did. So it wasn't your brother" Jason had an alarmed look, or maybe it was shear confusion.

"You heard him say that, Jason?"

"Yes. I followed you downstairs this morning, stood listening in the hallway."

Brendan pulled the boy to him and hugged him close. "So you know why Detective Segura and Frank are visiting Uncle Arnold? And why we're there?"

"Come on, Dad! I may be a kid, but I'm not stupid."

At that point Mrs. Serbein came from inside; at least Brendan assumed the middle-aged woman was Henry's wife. "Hello, Mrs. Serbein," he said cheerfully. "I'm so sorry to intrude on your privacy. I know you've had a difficult time."

215

"I just told them to get back on the road, Martha. So you can go back to your work."

But Martha chose to ignore her husband. "Oh, hush, Henry," she said. "I overheard part of what that little boy said. And this man doesn't look like he means us any harm. You're not with any media company, are you?"

"No, Ma'am, I'm not. And I'll not take up much of your time, I promise. My name is Brendan Carlson. I live over in Clackamas County, south of Portland. This is my son, Jason."

Jason disarmed old Henry completely by saying, "A pleasure to meet you Mrs. Serbein. You too, sir." He went over to shake their hands and Mrs. Serbein smiled at him. Henry took the offered hand briefly, but his scowl softened only a little.

"Come on over here and sit down on the porch," Martha said warmly. "I can see you have an important reason for being here, and to tell you the truth, I can use a little rest from what I was doing. Call me Martha. This old grump is Henry, and his bark is far worse than his bite."

Brendan had made up his mind that the barn he could partly see was exactly like the one in his vision. That, and the powerful smell of rotting onions had him convinced that in this house, days before, Bryan had indeed raped and killed a young blond woman.

"Thank you, Martha. You too Henry." Brendan sat down on the old upholstered couch, and he turned to see if Jason was with him. But the boy and the dog had found each other. Frosty had rolled over on his back and Jason was rubbing his belly, which seemed to please the dog immensely.

"He'll put up with that for no longer than a week," Henry said. "Why don't you go around the back with him, young feller. There's a rough lawn back there, and you'll find his ball. He'll fetch that old ball as many times as you can throw it."

The dog seemed to understand exactly what his master had suggested, and he sprang to his feet and pranced from side to side excitedly, woofing gently. Jason ran around the side of the house with Frosty at his side.

"I hardly know where to begin my story," Brendan said. "But my brother, a man I never even knew existed until a little over a year ago, escaped from prison several days ago. He has killed some people, and I... I didn't tell you, he's my identical twin. Anyway, I sometimes get dreams and psychic visions of what he's doing. I wish I didn't, and I wish I'd never heard of him, but sometimes what I see helps the police."

"You're a psychic, then? Is that what you're saying, Brendan?" Mrs. Serbein seemed fascinated, her eyes were wide in obvious amazement and she sat forward on the edge of her seat. Henry's frown showed his skepticism.

"In a way, I suppose I am a psychic. But not all the time, and only in connection with Bryan Olmstead. And even that didn't start happening until about two years ago. In fact I didn't even know he existed when they first occurred, so... Anyway, it scared the heck out of me, at the time."

"So what does all this have to do with us?" Henry still wanted no part of this conversation, wanted this stranger and his son gone.

"Well, sir, three days ago I had a vision, a waking vision of a young woman being killed inside a farm house. There was the strong smell of onions, like now, and I could see your barn. I could also see a wagon, loaded with yellow tarps. It doesn't seem to be there right now, but that's the only real difference. Anyway, the police said the DNA they found on the girl didn't match that of Bryan Olmstead, so that had me totally confused. I just had to come here and see if this really is the place. I'm very sorry to intrude, but I had to come."

There was an uncomfortable silence for what seemed like an eternity. Then, Martha said quietly, "Would you like to see inside, Brendan. Would that help?"

Brendan hesitated, wondering how he would react to seeing what would undoubtedly still be a bloodstained floor. But he silently nodded, and Martha led him inside.

It was a simple house, probably more than a hundred years old, and they entered directly into the living room. Everything seemed perfectly normal here, with old-fashioned furniture, but it was clean, tidy and undisturbed. Mingled with the smell of onions from outside, however, there were other odors Brendan recognized. There was a cleaning product smell, with a pine fragrance, but another that seemed sickly and cloying. Brendan instinctively knew that is was the smell of blood and death, and he tried to ignore it as Martha led him to the dining room. Following close behind was the silent Henry.

"They wouldn't let us touch anything until yesterday morning," Martha said apologetically. "We were called back here three days ago and we stayed in a motel for one night. We were in Nebraska when this happened, visiting family. Right here is where they found the body." She pointed, and Brendan noticed the glisten of tears in Martha's eyes. Henry looked sad as a bloodhound, too, but still he said nothing.

"We've cleaned up the floor as best we can, for now, but they took the rug away. We don't want it back again, anyway. It was heavily stained by blood, you know."

"Was it predominantly green, with geometric patterns in beige and red?"

Martha stared hard at Brendan, and then she nodded, evidently moved by the evidence that Brendan really was psychic. "Yes," she said. "It was. You mean you actually saw the rug in your vision?"

"I sure did. I saw this furniture, these windows..." He looked out through the dining room windows, toward the barn. "But what happened to the trailer out there? I saw a trailer with yellow tarps piled on it."

Martha looked at Henry in an odd way and said, "That's where we found the other body; buried in the tarps. He was–"

"Other body?" Brendan was flabbergasted. "There was another body?"

"Actually, it was Frosty that found it. He went crazy over there from the moment we got back home. I don't know if he could smell something, or if he sensed it some other way, but he made a heck of a fuss. Henry climbed up on the tarps and saw some blood, but when he moved some of them, there it was: the body."

"You said it was a he?"

Martha nodded. "You didn't see that part? They tell us the murdered young man either somehow interrupted what was going on here, or was perhaps taking part in it. The other man... I don't know, but they think maybe your brother... he probably killed this one and buried him in the tarps. God only knows why."

Brendan was deeply puzzled by this discovery. "Did you know the DNA they found on the girl was not my brother's? That's what they told me."

"Yes, they told us that too; so it might be from this other man."

Brendan's confusion came from the fact that he had envisioned the whole series of brutal assaults as if he, himself, was the perpetrator. Surely he could not have envisioned such acts by anyone other than his identical twin. Or could he?

"Do you mind if I go outside and look around?" he asked. "I'll not take long. And we should be getting back on the road real soon, anyway."

Martha showed Brendan down a hallway to the back door of the house. She opened the door and said, "Just toot your horn when you leave, no need to come back inside. Here, give your little boy this piece of candy." She reached into a pocket on her apron and pulled out a wrapped toffee and gave it to Brendan. He thanked her and stepped outside into the bright sunshine. It had been a little dingy inside, the windows being few and small in size, so it took a second or two for his eyes to adjust. He expected to see Jason and Frosty out here, playing on the Serbein's unkempt lawn, but there was no sign of them.

"Jason!" Brendan yelled. "Time to go, son." He waited, but there was no response. He shouted the boy's name again; louder this time. Still no answer.

The back door of the house opened up again, and Henry Serbein stepped outside, immediately assessing the situation. He glanced at Brendan and then placed two fingers between his lips and whistled, loud and long, a single shrill tone that carried far. Henry scanned the yard near the barn, and then he looked at Brendan again. "Frosty always comes," he said. "Never known him to go too far to hear me whistle. Come on, let's go see if we can find them."

Serbein led the way over to the barn and opened up the big sliding doors. They had been open just a few inches. "That's odd," he said. "I'm certain these doors were fully closed."

"Jason!" Brendan shouted as they entered. He was now starting to feel a dread fear..

"Hey, look," Henry said, pointing. "There's Frosty. Come on." He ran to the far end of the barn, where he could see part of his dog, lying motionless in the straw, his rear end protruding from a stall. "Oh, God, no!" He dropped to his knees and stared at Frosty as if he had seen the most awful sight. In fact he had! Frosty's throat had been slashed, and he lay on the bloody straw, lifeless and almost headless.

Brendan stood aghast. For several seconds he just stood there, shocked, transfixed by what he could see in the dim light. "Who could have done this thing?" he said, horrified. But then he turned, quickly surveying the interior of the barn. "Jason," he

221

yelled as loud as he could, now fearing that the dog and his son might have shared the same fate. "Jason!"

There was a loft in the barn. Brendan climbed the ladder and looked around. He could see that the many yellow tarpaulins had been stacked away, but there was no sign of his boy. He yelled again and again, his emotional state now near panic. He rushed down the ladder and outside he circled the barn, all the time yelling his Jason's name, now with tears streaming down his face. *What should he do?*

"Did your boy do this to my dog?"

Totally distraught, and nearly beyond rational thought, Brendan barely heard the words from behind him. He turned slowly and faced the angry looking Henry Serbein, standing just inside the barn door.

"What the hell are you saying, man?" Brendan hissed. "My son would never kill anything, especially a beautiful dog. How could you even think–?"

"Listen, I never seen you before in my life, so I don't know what you would do; you or your boy. But you tell me your twin brother is a brutal killer, and you show up here three days after these awful murder..." Brendan now noticed that Henry had a large scythe in his hand, was brandishing it menacingly. The rest of whatever Henry Serbein had to say was lost on Brendan, his emotions were taking over like a raging storm. He turned and ran, straight for his car. He knew he needed help. The police, maybe? Detective Segura? Frank Dobson, or Arnold Towncraft? No, all too far away. He needed immediate help. Either Henry Serbein would attack him or whoever had taken the life of

Serbein's dog would. But if he could just get to his car... On-Star. He would lock himself inside, push the On-Star emergency button and back out of the driveway far enough to be safe. Besides, he had the handgun Segura had lent him. It was under the seat of his car. Yes, he would take the gun and use it if necessary; defend himself against Serbein or deal with whoever had taken Jason.

All these thoughts raced through Brendan's mind as he ran the short distance to his car. Once there, he wrenched open the door and climbed in. He immediately locked the door and realized that Henry Serbein had not followed him. He relaxed a little, catching his breath.

"At last we meet, my dear brother."

Brendan froze. These words, spoken slowly and in a mere whisper, just behind his head, made his heart descend like a lead weight dropping inside his chest cavity. He instantly knew that Bryan had somehow made his way here and was now in his car, right behind him. Bryan had killed Henry Serbein's dog, and... and what the hell had he done with Jason? He started to turn, but he felt the cold steel of a gun barrel press against the back of his neck.

"Don't move a muscle."

There was a long and painful silence.

"I have your boy, Brendan, and he's alive. But he'll not be alive for long."

"You... What do you want, Bryan? Kill me if you like, but leave my boy alone, damn you."

223

"Oooh. Such brave talk. You really want to die, my darling brother? Just start the car and drive out of this stinking hell-hole. When you get out to the road, turn left. Do it!"

The gun barrel was thrust firmly into the base of Brendan's skull, and he reacted quickly. "The Serbein's are going to call the police," he said as he turned the ignition key. "They think I killed their dog, for sure, so they're bound to call the cops."

Bryan laughed. "Let 'em. You think the fuzz will see any need to rush out here for the sake of a dead dog? I'll be long gone before they show up. And you'll be turning cold."

"What have you done with my son?"

"He's safe, for now. There, turn down that dirt lane."

Brendan did as he was told, his mind racing. Dare he reach for the gun? He dangled his hand between his legs as far as he could and immediately realized he would need to bend forward to have any chance of reaching the weapon. If he did that... he dreaded the thought. But he had to do something. His mind was searching for something to say that would make a difference, or something to do that would give him a chance of overpowering his insane brother. He toyed with reaching up to make an adjustment to the rear-view mirror. If he did that he could push the On-Star emergency button. He had used it only once before, and he didn't remember what the response would be. Would there be a mechanical voice, like the one that responded to the hands-free phone, or would a live person come on? What would Bryan do if he heard either one? *He didn't risk it.*

They came to a small copse of trees, beyond which Brendan saw a dilapidated  structure, a small old barn that was ready to fall down. As they approached, he spotted a white automobile inside. It was the white Toyota he'd seen earlier. *So it was him!*

"How did you get here, Bryan?"

"Shut up and pull alongside that barn. Right there, on the far side, where we'll be hidden from the main road."

Brendan doubted that the barn itself could be seen from the road, much less an automobile. The crops growing in these fields were high, and there was also a slight rise they had climbed. But he did as he was told. "So how did you get here?" he asked again.

Bryan cackled. "The phone call fooled you all, huh? I knew it would. I gave the cell phone away, paid a guy in Redding to call your friend's house at a certain time. I knew where you were all the time; you, Towncraft, the detective and the other guy."

Brendan turned off the engine, waiting for his next instruction. "How do you know about them?" he asked.

"You're about to die, Brendan. What do you care how I know?"

"You get visions, don't you, Bryan? In your visions and dreams you see me, and you know what I'm doing sometimes."

"Yeah, I do. And I know that's how you tracked me down, last time. That's why I had to create some false impressions. The phone call from Redding, somebody else's DNA in the girl I did here. I'm clever, you know. I always knew I

225

was clever. Even our bitch of a mother told me how clever I was."

"Where's Jason, Bryan? I need to see that my son is safe." Brendan's tone sounded threatening, and it was deliberate. He hoped, though he realized the hope was a faint one, that his brother might feel some empathy for him. But Bryan seemed to pay no attention.

"When I was a kid, I used to see myself–I thought it was me–being treated real nice by a lovely woman. Emily was her name. She loved me a great deal, this Emily, but it was just a dream. I had vivid dreams like that all the time. She would–"

"Emily was my mother, Bryan. My adoptive mother." Brendan glanced in the rear-view mirror and saw Bryan wipe saliva away from his chin. He noticed a slight downturn on one side of his mouth. It looked a bit as if Bryan might have suffered a stroke, or maybe nerve damage. Other than that imperfection, and something indefinable in the eyes, he could be looking at his own reflection. He shuddered a little at the thought.

"Why were you the one to get adopted?" Bryan's voice now sounded shaky. *Was he softening?*

"I was just lucky, I guess. I had no idea you even existed. I honestly didn't. I had no boyhood dreams about you. Emily told me about you less than two years ago, and even more recently she told me she had tried to adopt you too, a year or so after me. But your mother... Sarah, she wouldn't let you go."

Bryan went very silent. Brendan checked the mirror again and he could see tears in the eyes he knew so well. Those eyes! They were his own eyes, but... different, harder, more pained.

Should he go for the gun now? He decided to try more softening-up; it seemed to be working. But Bryan spoke first.

"Sarah was a total bitch, Brendan. No, she was worse than that, and I hated her so bad. By the time I was five, she–"

"She abused you, didn't she?"

"Oh, yeah. Big time!"

Brendan thought he heard a sob. He waited a few seconds. "Did she beat you, Bryan? Was that it?"

The eyes in the mirror flashed with complex emotions. "Beat me? Oh, yeah. But that was–"

"What else did she do to you?" Brendan was burning with a powerful desire to know what had happened to Jason, where Bryan had hidden the boy, but he forced himself to stay on this current tack. "Did she abuse you in other ways?"

"Are you kidding me? See this scar on the top of my head? The bitch did that to me. She burned me with cigarette butts all the time. And see the way my mouth doesn't quite close right? Nerve damage, the doctor said. Permanent. I drool all the time like some kind of maniac. All the time."

Brendan was horrified at what he'd heard, but he also felt a powerful empathy, and this bothered him a great deal. He should feel nothing for this animal, and yet the emotions his brother was now reliving, in this bizarre stand-off, Brendan was also feeling deep inside him, as if he himself had known the torture Bryan had endured. He felt near to tears, and yet he knew he must remain strong... for Jason's sake. He took a chance:

"But you paid her back, didn't you?"

Bryan cackled again, and Brendan felt the pressure of the gun barrel on his neck ease off a little. He went for more progress on this dark, uncertain and heart-wrenching road: "What else did she do, brother?"

Again the slight sobbing sound. "She..."

"You can tell me, man. What did she do?"

"She would make me pleasure her."

Brendan felt a shudder of revulsion ripple down his spine.

"As a young boy, you mean?"

"Oh, yeah. Starting when I was six. It was–"

"But how? At age six?" Brendan turned without thinking as he said this, virtually forgetting his own predicament, staggered by what he was hearing. There was no response from Bryan at first, or from his gun; in fact the hand that gripped the weapon fell to Bryan's lap, and he sagged back into the rear seat of Brendan's Cadillac, seemingly exhausted by the memory of his childhood terrors.

Brendan eyed his brother for a while. He had the opportunity to reach for his own gun now, but the thought never occurred to him. He knew the depths of despair Bryan felt as a boy, could now sense the utter confusion and feelings of worthlessness Bryan must have felt at the time... and throughout his entire life.

"She made me pleasure her with my hands, with my mouth, and with this thing she had found somewhere; this carved... it was a carved wooden prick. And then she'd shove that same thing up my..."

Brendan felt like sobbing himself as he watched his brother suddenly descend into some dark place of incredible mental horror. He seemed to shrink physically, and he looked as if he could die from the anguish he suffered. Brendan was tempted to reach for the gun in Bryan's hand, but before he could make such a move, Brendan's eyes suddenly flashed and he sat up straight, brought the gun up again and placed the muzzle inside his own mouth.

"Bryan, don't!" yelled Brendan.

The report from the small caliber gun inside the closed space of Brendan's car was deafening, and Brendan felt a flood of emotion that engulfed him completely as life instantly left his brother's body. He felt as if he had also died, or some part of him had. He had no affection for this beast of a man, now dead on the seat behind him, and yet...

Jason! He had to find Jason. Adrenaline rushed through Brendan's body and enlivened him despite his deep melancholy, and he tore open his car door. Maybe Jason was inside the white Toyota? Or in the barn somewhere? *Oh, please God let him be alive!*

The Toyota was not locked, but a quick inspection showed no sign of his son inside. He slammed the door, and that was when he heard it: a slight sound. The trunk! Jason was in the trunk. He realized he would need a key, so he checked the ignition. Not there. He searched the dashboard for a trunk release button. There was none. *The keys must be in one of Bryan's pockets!*

Rushing now, afraid that Jason could be suffocating, he wrenched open the left side door of the Cadillac and couldn't help marveling at how little blood there was. Unlike in the movies, the bullet had not blown off the back of Bryan's head, scattering blood, brain and skull tissue all over the place. There was a mere trickle of blood from Bryan's mouth, and a little more from his nostrils, but that was it. Brendan felt for the keys and located them quickly. He rushed back to the Toyota and in his haste he dropped the keys to the ground. Recovering quickly, he soon had the trunk unlocked and he yanked it open.

*Thank you God! Jason is alive!*

The boy had been trussed up and gagged, using yards of duct tape. His eyes were streaming with tears of fear, or maybe the joy of seeing his father. Brendan tore off the tape from his son's mouth, and Jason sobbed, "Daddy."

Brendan hoisted the boy out of the trunk and hugged him, sobbing in relief. "I'm so sorry, Jase," he managed to say. "I am so sorry. I should never have brought you here." He smothered the boy's face with kisses, and then he sat him down on the ground, started to pull at the rest of his bindings.

Jason looked around, seeming predictably agitated and anxious. "Where is he, dad?"

Brendan stopped what he was doing for a second, realizing that Jason would have to know what Bryan had done, would see his lifeless body and the blood, the gun. "He's no longer a threat, son," he said, simply, trying to find a way to explain everything as he finished removing the last of the duct tape. He hugged Jason close again and said, "We're safe, Jase, and that's all that matters. I am so proud of you."

Jason's eyes flooded with tears again as he remembered something horrific. "He killed Frosty, Dad."

"You saw him do that?"

Jason nodded solemnly.

"He was a very bad man, Jason, and now he is dead."

"But he was your brother."

Brendan was shocked, and also amazed at the evident compassion his son felt, despite his awful experiences. He had hoped to keep his two young boys from knowing anything of the threat they had faced, and also to withhold details of who was threatening them; certainly keeping from them all the details of what kind of person might do such dreadful things to other people. But perhaps it was inevitable that they would find out.

"Yeah. He was my brother, but I never knew him, Jase. Not until today did I come to know him." Brendan's eyes were teary again as he thought of the dreadful way Bryan had been treated as a small innocent boy. "Some day, son, when you are old enough, I will tell you all about my brother, Bryan Olmstead. But right now we have to get you back to your own brother, and to your Mom."

"Where is he?"

Brendan hesitated. "He's in the car. You stay here for a minute or two, okay? I'll put him in the trunk, so you don't have to see him."

"I want to see him." Jason's eyes were clear and his voice resolute.

"What? Jason, I don't think that's—"

"I want to see him again, Dad. I'm not scared."

Brendan couldn't understand Jason's request, but he honored it anyway. In fact, the young boy helped his father load the body of Bryan Olmstead into the trunk of the car, taking his dead uncle's feet while his father lifted the heavy end of the body. Jason quietly watched as his father gently placed a blanket under Bryan's head, and he knew it was mostly to prevent blood staining the trunk carpeting. But he also seemed to understand why this dead man was being treated gently.

Brendan climbed into the driver's seat and turned to his son, seated next to him. "Have you any idea how much I love you, Jason?" he said. He then pulled the boy to him again and squeezed him hard and long.

"I do, Dad."

"What?"

"I know how much you love me, or us."

Brendan looked at Jason for the longest time, realizing just how close they had both come to being killed. He released his boy slowly and smiled at him, not able to say all that was in his heart. He reached forward to start the car, and Jason pointed at his arm.

"You have blood on your sleeve, Dad," he said.

Brendan turned his arm, and sure enough Jason was right. He reached behind him for a tissue, knowing the smear of blood would be permanent if he didn't remove it.

"That's your brother's blood, Dad," Jason said solemnly.

"Yeah, it must be." Brendan decided not to worry about the small stain on his sleeve. It was an old shirt anyway.

He smiled at his son, now seeming so brave and mature. It was an odd smile, and he really felt like crying. He had never known such deep and mixed emotions in his life; and he silently prayed he never would again. He turned on the ignition and pushed the small steering wheel button that activated his On-Star phone.

"On-Star Ready."

"Dial," Brendan said.

Brendan then stated, one digit at a time, the string of numbers that would connect him to Arnold Towncraft's home, and he waited, knowing this would be one terribly difficult phone call.

## Chapter Twenty-Two

Arnold took the call in his bedroom-where he was looking for nail scissors, having broken a fingernail, so the other two men didn't hear any part of the startling conversation he had with Brendan. It was lengthy, and mostly one-sided. Brendan calmly told all that he'd learned. Arnold hung up and rushed downstairs, found Frank and Segura in the kitchen. They were making plans for what they assumed might happen when Bryan Olmstead showed up. "Come and join us, Arnold," Frank said cheerfully.

"It's over," Arnold said. "Bryan Olmstead is dead; he took his own life."

There was a stunned silence, both men staring at Arnold, incredulous.

"Who called?" Segura asked.

"Brendan. Bryan followed him from up here somewhere, and–"

"Bryan was here? How can that be?"

"He gave the cell phone to someone, paid them to make that call from Redding, earlier this morning." Arnold sat down and seemed to sag with exhausted relief. "He also planted somebody else's DNA on the girl, apparently. The girl he killed in Madras."

"So it was him!"

Arnold nodded solemnly. The story told by Brendan had shocked him deeply, and he felt slightly nauseated at what he'd heard.

"Has Brendan called the police? What's going on?" Segura was agitated, anxious to hear more.

"Bryan blew his brains out, in the back seat of Brendan's car," Arnold said. "Brendan's bringing the body back here, didn't want the local cops involved, thought they would keep him there unreasonably. Decided you could handle everything from here, Art" Arnold looked quizzically at the detective. "Did he do the right thing?"

"Yeah, he did. But I'd better get a Medical Examiner here, and the locals. How long?"

"Huh? Oh, they'll be back here in an hour or so."

Frank asked, "Are Brendan and the boy all right."

"All right?" Arnold paused. "They are physically okay, if that's what you mean. Let me tell you what I know, and then I'll go over and get Kathy, Rebecca and Tommy."

"I tell you what, Arnold," Segura said. "Let's not be in a hurry to bring the women back here. My guess is that it'll take a while for the ME to finish his work, and no doubt the local sheriff will need to ask me and Bryan a whole lot of questions. Let the women stay right where they are until the fuss dies down. In fact, why don't you go over to the motel, tell them Bryan is no longer a threat, and that Brendan is delayed a little but will be on his way home soon. That way, they can relax a little longer at the motel, and maybe later you can take them all out for dinner. Bring them back here around eight tonight. I should be gone by then, and everything here should have settled back to normal."

"Normal, Art?" Arnold snorted. "That seems... You're heading home tonight?"

"Yeah. I'll have a ton of paperwork to do when I get back. Reports up the ying-yang. You wouldn't believe the B.S. I'll have to go through; especially with all this happening up here." Segura grinned. "And then I'll be on the carpet, no doubt."

"Well, you have my offer, Art," Arnold said. "I'm dead serious."

Segura went quiet for a few seconds. He eyed Arnold oddly, and then he said, "Yeah, I know you are. Let me get done what I have to do, and then we'll talk about that offer some more, okay?"

Arnold nodded. "How long before you know all the details of what Bryan did before he got here?"

"We may never know everything, but I'll tell you all that I learn within a couple of days, how's that? Brendan's time with Olmstead seems to have revealed some important facts. Why don't you tell us everything he told you?"

So Arnold recounted what Brendan had told him over the phone, and both Frank and Segura interrupted many times with questions. Most of them Arnold could not answer and, it turned out, an hour later, many of these same questions Brendan couldn't answer, either.

## Epilog.

### Eight Days Later

"That must be Art Segura," Arnold said, hearing the crunch of tires on the driveway. He arose to greet the detective, turning to Kathleen and adding, "Now you know why I don't ever want to pave that driveway."

Kathy grinned. "They have electronic devices that will announce a visitor, dear."

"Humbug! I hate electronic devices."

"Really? And you intend to go into the private eye business? Go meet your new partner, you old goat. Maybe he'll be a little more interested in keeping up with today's miraculous inventions."

Arnold headed for the front door without a response. He admitted the smiling Segura, who greeted Kathy from the hallway as he removed his shoes. It was raining outside.

"What have I done?" he said. "Does it rain all the time up here?"

"Pretty much," Towncraft said. "But you'll get used to it. Can I pour you something?"

They entered the living room, where Kathy sat doing needlework. "Don't get up Kathy," Segura said, and he bent over to kiss her cheek. "I see you're into sherry. I'll have one too, if I may, Arnold."

"Good flight up, Art?" Kathy asked as the detective seated himself.

"Not bad. A little bumpy on final approach. There's a lot of disturbed air all over the place. Late summer storms coming up, mostly over the Sierras. Quite a show."

Arnold returned with a clean sherry glass and the decanter. He poured one for Segura and topped-up his own. Kathy declined the offer of more.

"Let's toast our mutual success," Arnold said, and the three raised their glasses. "I am so pleased you accepted my offer, Art. It's going to be fun."

"Your timing was spectacular, Arnold. I was ready. When do we start?"

"We have already started, my friend. Today is the first of September, and I have your paycheck for the first three months." He reached into his coat pocket and pulled out a sealed envelope. "Is it okay if I pay you three months in advance each time?"

Segura grinned his reply. "Well, I can put up with that, I suppose. But do we actually have something to get started on? A case of some sort?"

"As a matter of fact, we do. But I'll get into that later. First, I want to hear everything you have learned about the Bryan Olmstead case in the last few days."

"Oh, dear," Kathy said. "I'm not sure I want to hear all the gory details. I think I'll go do some work in the greenhouse." She downed the last of her sherry and departed.

Arnold was pleased she had gone. He'd hoped she would; they had discussed the matter before Segura's arrival. "You think all the answers are in, Art?"

"Pretty much. But you know most of it, really."

"Okay, but what was the significance of the man Bryan killed at the Serbein farm?"

"Aah. Bryan was simply trying to be cute at that point; though 'cute' is hardly the word for it. That young man was a known gay prostitute named Seth Thompson. Bryan apparently picked him up in a bar, paid him well to take the trip with him from the Sacramento area up to Madras. It's evident that he had Thomas use a condom and... sorry, Arnold, but he had anal sex with Bryan. This provided the DNA for Bryan to plant on the girl." Segura paused, expecting the genteel and gentlemanly professor to recoil. It didn't happen, so he continued: "Then he killed Thompson and hid his body in a pile of canvas tarps."

"Aaah, I see. So Bryan planted Thompson's DNA inside the poor girl he killed at the Serbein farm. Presumably, he used another condom when he raped the girl, so that was the confusing element. But why would he bother to do all this? He must have known you guys were onto him, right?"

Segura chuckled. "He sure did. But that's just the point. He simply wanted to mess with our minds. He's a clever bastard, and he just wanted to prove it. Maybe he *needed* to prove it."

"So he came all the way up to Madras and killed, just to throw a scare into us at that stage of the game. Then, having made sure the DNA he planted would prove to be someone else's, but not for several days, he went back south again. But why?"

Segura sipped his sherry before responding. "You used the word, 'game,' and I suspect you're right, Arnold. This is pure speculation on my part, so I can't be certain of any of it, but I think Bryan wanted his last acts to be killing Brendan and is family. You and Frank too, if he could, but especially Brendan and Rebecca. But he had mischief in mind, and he had other vile appetites to satisfy, as you know. So I think, when he got close to here, and to his ultimate goal, he knew that once Bryan was dead there would be little reason to go on living. He decided to go off and indulge himself in his other sport: brutalizing women for some sort of depraved satisfaction... or perhaps a generalized revenge"

"So he went back down into California believing you would be certain he was up here; at least for a few days. That would give him time to– How many did he kill in those three days?"

"As far as we know, there were just the two you knew about, in Redding and in the Bay Area."

"So how many in total?"

"Counting the four that he killed the first time, before his escape a few days ago? Fourteen. No, fifteen including Seth Thompson. Thirteen women, two children and one man. But he may have been doing things like this for years, moving around

240

the way he did. We can't trace much of his activity, so who knows how many of the missing young women of Arizona, Nevada, Colorado..."

"And his victim list would include Brendan and Jason, if– God, do you think he would have actually killed his own brother if Brendan hadn't taken the approach that he did? Getting him to talk about his awful experiences as a child."

Segura sighed deeply. "We'll never know that, will we?"

"The mind is a remarkable instrument, Art. But it is really quite fragile when we're young. When Brendan told me what his brother had endured, I... Well, I just couldn't believe it."

"Man's inhumanity is sometimes beyond awful, Arnold." Segura laughed sardonically. "Women's too," he added.

"And that's why you wanted out of your job, I suppose. You ever see a case like this before?"

"No, never a bloody rampage like this one, or a case of child abuse quite like Bryan's. Bad stuff. Child abuse often seems to turn people into freaky animals, sure, but never exactly like this." Segura paused. "You spoken with Frank since he left?"

"Yes, I have. Twice. He took this case hard, too. He's sick, you know; has Lou Gherig's disease." Arnold watched for a response from his companion, and he sure got one.

"Oh, God, no."

Arnold nodded, feeling close to losing his emotions at the thought of his uncle's imminent suffering. "Yeah. My sentiments exactly," he managed to say.

"How long does he have? Do they know?"

"It's a guess. Three years, maybe four. But he'll be virtually incapacitated much sooner. That's why I want him nearby. He and Hilda are going to live next door as soon as they can sell their home back east. I'll hire professional help for them as soon as needed. By the way, he made me promise not to tell anyone about his illness, so act surprised if he tells you, okay?"

Segura grunted, struggling with his own emotions. "How about Brendan? You've spoken with him?"

"Sure. Every day since he returned home. He's doing okay, considering everything he went through."

"I just can't imagine."

"You and me both. More sherry?"

Segura said he could use more, and Arnold topped up both glasses.

"There seems to be one good development, Art. For Brendan, that is."

Segura looked puzzled; perhaps having difficulty figuring what kind of good might have come from realizing the bestiality of his own brother, and hearing of the horrors of Bryan's childhood.

"Brendan had no more visions of his brother's activities after the one killing near Madras. The other three took place without him even knowing about it. And even when Bryan held Jason captive, Brendan had no inkling. This was his own son!"

Segura understood exactly what Arnold was saying. "So he feels he no longer tormented by that sort of psychic ability. Is that what you mean?"

"Exactly. But he saw it not as an ability, more like a liability, or a curse."

"But that same liability may have helped him reach his wife when she was in a coma, and it certainly led to the arrest of his brother. Twice!"

Arnold nodded solemnly. "True enough. But now he is released, he believes, from ever having those sorts of nightmares again. Imagine how good that feels, just knowing that weird potential is gone."

"Well, his maniac of a brother is dead, has burned in hell by now, so Brendan would never have made contact with him again, anyway, right?"

Arnold had an odd expression on his face. "Can you be sure of that, Art? I mean, Brendan believes in God, and in heaven and hell. If he thought there was some chance that he could make contact with his brother again, especially from the depths of hell, can you imagine what going to sleep each night would be like for him?"

Segura gulped at the realization of what Arnold was saying. "I see what you mean about being released," he said. "You're right. That would be good news."

"About your comment that Bryan was a maniac, Art. There's something I'd like to say about that. Maniac? Maybe, he was, but who is to say what terrors Bryan Olmstead endured? Who among us can condemn him for his brutal acts without also feeling sad for him, knowing what we now know. And there may well have been more, much more. What little we know came out in the short space of a few minutes in a bizarre conversation with a brother he had not seen since they were babies. He spent his adult life seeking his own meaning in life–his own answers–because, as a boy, all he had been dealt was hatred, scorn, pain and degradation. What should have been the loving embrace of his mother became, instead, a hellish maelstrom of confusion and torment. He turned out to be a beastly killer, that's for certain, but he was also a victim. Life dealt him no cards at all in a game he could never win. I grieve deeply for all of his victims, of course, but also for Bryan himself. He never had a chance, poor bastard."

Arnold looked up and noticed the glisten of tears in the eyes of his new partner, who raised his glass and said, "I'm going to enjoy working with you, boss. You are the most understanding and sensitive man I ever met. You must have had a perfect set of parents, yourself, I'd guess."

Arnold merely smiled as he joined the toast. He did not respond, but he knew full well that many years and much love had rescued him from an abysmal childhood of his own, and he felt fortunate that he had not ended up like Bryan Olmstead.